CHAPTER 1

*L*ana poked her head in through the back screen door. "I come bearing gifts." A basket lined with a pink linen napkin and adorned with a polka dot ribbon followed her head. "My yummy nut date bars." She stepped inside.

I was already halfway across the kitchen to the basket. I reached in to grab a gooey bar, Lana's own concoction of chewy dates, peanut butter and whatever goodies she had in her kitchen pantry.

"Hmm, it's still warm. Are those pistachio nuts I'm tasting?"

"Yep and chunks of chocolate, but you already know that because you have a sixth sense when it comes to chocolate." Lana walked straight to the coffee pot. She had recently decided to high-light her brunette hair with streaks of pale silver in an attempt to camouflage the emerging strands of gray. I still wasn't sure how I felt about the style change.

I placed the basket on the large pine table in the center of kitchen. The Cider Ridge Inn's kitchen was easily my favorite spot in the massive house. The dogs seemed to agree. Newman and

Redford were stretched out in front of the giant brick hearth. It wore the wonderful patina of age and use. The original black kettle still hung over the spit. I had yet to use the two hundred year old cooking hearth but its restoration was on my list of a million other projects to bring the inn up to code and make it a welcome place for visitors. That dream was still a long way off, however, making my current day job as a journalist for the *Junction Times* a necessity.

"I'm just about to head to work." I reached into the basket and pulled out two more bars, one for my coffee break and one for Myrna, my favorite work mate. "I suppose I should ask why my sister has baked me a basket of my favorite date bars."

Lana batted her lashes innocently as she took a sip of coffee. She released a 'hmm coffee' sigh as she lowered the cup. "Why can't I just make something nice for my favorite sister?" A fabulously fake smile followed.

"Well, if this basket had arrived by way of my little sister, Emi, then I wouldn't think twice about it or even question the motive. But when my big sister skips in with a wonderful treat, it usually means she's about to ask me to fill three hundred goodie bags for an upcoming party event." I lifted my right hand. "I still have paper cuts from the four hundred origami swans I helped you fold for the Richman wedding. By the way, I'm folding those things in my dreams and the other day I absently folded my napkin into a swan while I was eating a sandwich at Layers. Fortunately, Raine, my lunch mate understood and sympathized. She said she can't look at a square of toilet paper without wondering how it would look with wings."

Lana lingered over a few more sips of coffee. "I just need to ask you one little favor."

"Ah ha, I knew it. These yummy bars came with a price." I broke off another piece. "Out with it. You've come this far and I'm not handing these back so what is it you need? Counting Jordan

MURDER AT THE INN

FIREFLY JUNCTION COZY MYSTERY #3

LONDON LOVETT

WILD FOX PRESS

almonds for treat bags? Folding paper stars for garlands? Stringing lights around the barn?"

"Hosting a small group for a night in the Cider Ridge Inn."

A sharp laugh shot from my mouth. "Funny lady."

"Actually, I'm serious." Lana's chin jutted forward, signaling that she was switching to her persuasive salesperson mode. There were few people on earth who could resist a Lana Taylor sales pitch. It was the secret behind her success. "It's a charming little group called the—" she smiled enthusiastically. "You're going to love this. They are known as the Applegate Paranormal Preservation Society." Before I could interject or toss out an objection she held up her finger. "Wait. There's more. Their motto is—" Her brown eyes lifted in thought, then she pulled out her phone. "I want to get this exactly right because it's so awesome." I'd already given up the fight and glanced at the clock on the wall while she pulled up the *awesomeness* on her phone. "Here it is. They call themselves APPS for short and they are—" She cleared her throat. Only Lana could make this big of a production out of something as silly as a club motto. "APPS is dedicated to helping spirits lead full un-lifes." She chuckled. "Get it? Un-lifes."

"Never heard such a clever play on prefixes and words." Sarcasm dripped off my response. "Lana, you must be out of your mind. The inn is so far from ready for visitors, there's just no possible way."

"But that's why they want to stay here. Cider Ridge Inn is on some important paranormal ghost hunter list as one of the most haunted homes in the region. The creepier, more dilapidated and creakier, the better. Look, it's one night. I'll bring all the food and amenities. You just need to provide the inn and any of those spirits that might be lurking in the crumbling walls and rafters." She winked dramatically as if we were both part of a two person society of skeptics. Lana didn't believe in ghosts and neither had I until Edward Beckett, the resident ghost, made his first introduction.

My gaze circled the kitchen. Usually by now, this topic would have already conjured my incorporeal friend, but I didn't see or hear him.

Lana walked to the sink to wash her cup. "I'd hate to think that the Dandelion Inn over in Birch Highlands was going to get all the publicity and recognition as a haunted inn. They are staying at the Dandelion on their second night and I don't think that place is half the haunted character as this one. But if you want Dandelion Inn to become the cool place to visit, then that's your choice."

I snuffled an 'oh pleeze' sound. "As if I ever had a choice in this matter once you made up your mind that it would happen."

She put the cup in the drying rack and spun around. "So you'll let them stay?"

"I'm not happy about the idea but I know if I say no you'll stay here and bug me until I say yes and I'm late for work."

The pots and pans hanging from the rack over the pine table swung into each other, creating a light tinny clatter. It seemed I'd found my ghost.

Lana stared up in confusion at the pots that were still in pendulum motion. "What caused that to happen?"

I was constantly having to drum up excuses for unexplained events. "Occasionally a breeze shoots through the back screen door."

Lana reached up and stopped one of the pots from moving. "Must have been a good strong breeze to move aluminum and iron pots. Sometimes, it almost seems as if you *do* have a spirit hanging around the inn. A few of those weird occurrences should be perfect for their visit. They'll be thrilled."

"How many people can I expect?"

"Just five."

"Really?" I was starting to smell an ulterior motive. "You don't usually bother with small parties of five. What's in this for you?"

Lana picked at some invisible specks on the pine table. "It might lead to something more substantial and lucrative."

"Substantial and lucrative," I repeated. "Now that sounds more like my sister Lana."

She sighed loudly. "All right so I'm doing this as a favor to show the group that I'm the perfect party planner for the annual October Paranormal Society Convention. Every year the ghost hunter groups get together for a big shindig and this year they are considering Firefly Junction. It would be a great gig."

"Fine. But you're going to owe me more than just a basket of date bars." My phone buzzed. I picked it up from the counter. "Oh shoot, I forgot the electrician was coming this morning."

"Then you decided to rewire the house first? I guess that's why I don't hear Ursula's incessant harping this morning," Lana said.

"Yes, they have a few weeks off. They had some small job over in Hickory Flats and yes, I hate to admit it but I'm looking forward to the break. Not that I'm kidding myself. The electrical upgrade is going to cost me a fortune but Henry was right, I need to have the electrical wiring brought up to modern code before we go any further with the restoration. Guess it's a good thing you delayed me or I might have missed him."

"See, big sister to the rescue as always," Lana quipped as she headed to the back door.

"Oh really? Think you have that backwards this time. When can I expect the apples?"

Lana laughed. "APPS and they will be here tomorrow night." She blurted the last part quickly before walking out.

I lunged toward the door and swung it open as she hurried down the steps.

"Tomorrow night? Thanks for all the advanced notice."

She waved over her shoulder without looking back.

"Your sister is pushy," Edward's deep drawl rolled around the vast kitchen.

I shut the back door and turned around. He was standing, (as well as someone made of vapor could stand) beneath the hanging rack of pots and pans shifting them back and forth with his long, transparent fingers. The gentle clanging sounds produced reminded me of the pulleys on boats moored in an agitated harbor. The blue ribbon holding the queue of hair at Edward's neck was always tied perfectly in a bow. His cravat, the one article of clothing that had been loosened while he lay dying from a gunshot wound, always hung in exactly the same position around his neck. The shiny black Hessian boots, the ones that were too difficult to remove on his death bed, hovered just above the kitchen floor as he tapped the pots one more time, sending them into a metallic chorus.

"Please stop playing music on my pots and pans. By the way, I need you to be on your best behavior today. An electrician will be here for the next week working on wiring throughout the house."

He turned around and leaned against the pine table, crossing the boots at his ankles. It was a casual stance that always made him look alive and solid, even though his feet weren't touching the ground. "What a lot of bother. Candles and a few gas lanterns are all that's needed to light up this house."

"And to set it on fire too," I added. "I think we'll stick with electricity. Beeswax gives me a headache and I just don't see myself walking around every night with a candlestick in my hand."

"Did your sister suffer some sort of shock?"

"What do you mean?"

His lighter than air fingers fluttered toward his own dark head of hair. "Those white streaks in her hair. Did she experience some sort of fright?"

I laughed lightly. "No fright . . . unless you count a fear of looking forty."

6

Edward coasted over to check out the contents of Lana's goodie basket. "Looks like bricks of mud. Your sister brought you bricks of mud and you immediately caved to her demand that you allow strangers into the house."

"They aren't bricks of mud and I didn't cave. I compromised. And it's only for one night. Just make yourself scarce tomorrow night. Scratch that. Make yourself completely non-existent."

I had no other ghosts to compare him to, but Edward was particularly striking and handsome, a quality that caused him more trouble than good when he was of flesh and blood. His dark, appealing good looks were very much to blame for his untimely death when they proved too tempting for Bonnie Ross, the original lady of the house. An angry husband, Edward's distant cousin, no less, sent Edward to an early grave with a dueling pistol. Only that grave didn't seem to be able to hold him and he somehow ended up lingering in the hallways and empty rooms of the Cider Ridge Inn. His reason for staying behind was a mystery to both of us but I intended to find out one day. At least one day when I had a moment of free time.

A truck pulled up to the house. "The electrician is here. Go find something to keep yourself occupied today and stay out of his way. He came highly recommended and I don't need you scaring him off with your ghostly antics."

"Highly recommended? This from the woman who hired two court jesters to restore the house." With that, Edward vanished into thin air.

CHAPTER 2

om Fielding, the electrician, lumbered toward the front porch. Parker Seymour, my boss, had recommended him for the job of updating the wiring at the inn. Parker had a good belly laugh when he told me that Tom's nickname was Big Friendly Giant, like the character in the children's book. He also told me I'd see why when I met the man.

Tom had to duck to avoid crowning himself on the portico as he climbed the steps. A mound of light brown hair topped his broad head and was cut short enough to highlight his two enormous ears. His friendly gray eyes sparkled above a bulbous red nose, the perfect complement to his broad smile. My hand was completely swallowed up by his as he shook it.

"Miss Taylor? We talked on the phone. Tom Fielding." His baritone voice reminded me of the big bass drum in a marching band.

I tilted my head back to smile up at him. "I'm sure you get this question all the time—"

"Six foot seven," he answered quickly. "Although my mother

swears I was six foot eight when I graduated high school. I guess somewhere along the way I dropped an inch. Either way, it saves me time on a ladder. If you can show me to the basement where the electrical box is located, I can get started. I know you mentioned you'd be leaving for work this morning."

"Yes. Come on inside and I'll show you to the basement." As I opened the door, Newman and Redford bounded out. A tennis ball was jammed between Newman's fangs. Normally, a motor driven wench couldn't pry that ball from his teeth but my dog literally did a jaw drop when he saw the giant man on the porch. The tennis ball bounced down the steps, landing softly in the grass at the bottom. Both border collies sat obediently without even being told to sit.

Tom's laugh nearly rattled the windows and caused Redford to whine nervously. "Hello, you two." He leaned down and let both dogs smell his giant hand before giving each one a pat on the head.

"I hope you don't mind dogs. They generally just sleep out on the back porch and chase squirrels while I'm at work. They won't get in your way."

"I don't mind at all."

I led Tom into the house. He lowered his head to avoid the doorjamb. "These older houses tend to have a patchwork of various electrical systems. When was this place built?"

"Early nineteenth century." I led him through to the kitchen and to the cellar door. "I'm sure it was candles and lanterns for the first century." I thought about Edward's candle suggestion. He must have been 'in residence' when the first electricity was wired through the house. It must have been quite surprising for him to go from candle wicks to glowing light flicked on from a switch in the wall.

Poor Tom nearly had to walk on all fours down into the cramped basement with its low slung ceiling. I reached for the chain and pulled on the single light bulb. It flickered and instantly began to smell like burnt dust. "I'm afraid this is the only light down here. The fuse box is over there in the corner."

"I've brought my own lights. I spend a lot of time in dark basements." His laugh thundered off the block walls. "I suppose that sounds a little creepy," he continued. "But you understand what I mean."

"Of course." We turned past the rickety wooden staircase to the corner where the antiquated electrical box was sitting.

Tom spent a few moments clearing the cobwebs from around his head and then pulled a pair of wire-rimmed glasses from his shirt pocket. The wire temples were spread wide to fit around his large face. He leaned down and inspected the box, a black lacquer rectangle embossed with brassy gold print. "Ah ha, a Western. Oldie but goodie." He straightened. It was like watching a giraffe pull its head up off the ground. "I'll get started right away. I should be finished in a week as long as that old Cider Ridge ghost doesn't get in my way."

My eyes popped nearly as wide as my mouth. "Ghost?" I muttered shakily.

His laugh scared a rat out from hiding. It scurried across an overhead beam and disappeared into an opening in the wall. The rat temporarily took my mind off the ghost subject.

"Do you think there's any chance that the rat we just saw is a recluse? A loner?" I asked.

"You should probably call an exterminator just in case. And I was just kidding about the ghost, of course."

My sigh of relief was strong enough to blow dust off the fuse box. "Of course."

"The rumor of that ghost has been circulating around these parts for years. Just like the ghost of Lauren Grace over at the Dandelion Inn, it's just a lot of fluff being tossed around by people with more time on their hands than they know what to do with."

"Yes, I've heard the Dandelion Inn has a ghost too." I coughed. "I mean is supposed to be haunted too. I've got to get to work so I'll let you get started." I headed to the stairs.

"Is there anyone else in the house?"

My foot missed the first step. I grabbed the loose railing to keep from falling. "Anyone else?" I asked. He'd thrown me off with the ghost comment. I needed to pull myself together. It was the first time I'd left someone, other than Henry and Ursula, in the house alone. I worried what havoc my very real ghost may cause. "Oh right. No. Just me. So feel free to turn off the electricity. I made sure to unplug everything."

"Terrific."

I headed up the steps and was nearly clear of the house when Edward came out from the shadows on the front porch. The front porch was the outermost border to his eternal world.

"That's not a human," he said as he floated up onto the railing. "That's something out of Greek mythology."

"Just behave," I said sharply.

"What's that?" Tom asked as he walked out the front door.

"Oh, hello, nothing." I waved my hands in the air as if that helped me look less crazy. "Just talking to myself. Reminders of things I need to do today."

"Like behave," Edward said quietly behind me. My heart skipped a nervous beat, but then I reminded myself only I had the *privilege* of hearing him.

"Sorry to interrupt your mental list." Tom smiled and continued down the steps toward his truck.

I spun on my heels, lifted my hands and flexed my fingers open and shut silently telling Edward to vanish or disappear or dissipate, whatever process needed.

He stared at my hands. "I can't tell if this pantomime means you painted your nails with one of those garish colors again or if you're having some sort of seizure."

I grunted and stomped my foot.

"I'm going with the latter," he quipped. "I'm leaving but I'm not happy about having Goliath stomping around the house all day." His figure fizzled into thin air.

CHAPTER 3

$\mathcal{M}$yrna came gliding around the corner from the break room as I stepped into the newspaper office. She was holding a chocolate buttermilk donut on a napkin. "Morning, Sunni. Chase brought donuts." She stopped on the short journey to her desk and lowered her voice. "Of course, it was his turn."

"True. Did he remember jelly donuts?" I pulled the strap of my laptop case off my shoulder.

"Already put one on your desk." Myrna practically skipped away with her buttermilk confection. Myrna was only five feet tall with particularly short legs but she moved with the fluid grace of a ballerina. I'd talked her into taking dance lessons, assuring her she was a natural. It turned out she had always wanted to be a dancer but she'd convinced herself a dancer needed long legs. Two weeks ago she'd signed up for a ballroom dance class.

I lowered my laptop onto my slightly cluttered desk, making sure not to squish the jelly donut. "How was dance class last night?" I asked.

She chirped with excitement and scurried across the room to my desk. "Theodore, the dance instructor, told me I was his best pupil to date. His sister teaches a ballet class on Friday nights at the same studio. I'm thinking of joining." Myrna was trying a new orange color on her lips. It was bold and slightly distracting.

"You should join. Like I keep saying, you were born with a ballerina's grace."

"Aren't you the sweetest. And you were born with far too much journalistic talent to work in this newspaper office, but I'm glad you're here." She motioned back toward the editor's office. "Chase is in there now." She leaned down to whisper. "I think there's trouble in paradise if you catch my drift."

Which I didn't at first. I blinked up at her waiting for her to elaborate. "Paradise?"

"Chase and Rebecca are not speaking, apparently. Something about him always flirting too much with other women."

I took most of Myrna's gossip lightly. She loved to embellish and add her own details. Chase Evans, a writer for the *Junction Times*, was dating Rebecca Newsom, the newspaper owner's daughter. That relationship kept him billed as lead reporter even though our editor, Parker Seymour, often complained about the lack of depth and quality of his work. A twinge of guilt grabbed me as my mind immediately dashed to the possibility of a breakup resulting in some of the better stories landing in my lap. I quickly doused the guilt with a bite of jelly donut.

Myrna nodded at the donut. "Good stuff, eh? Anyhow, I think Parker wants to see you after he's done talking to Chase. There's been plenty of grumbling behind that door today so Chase is not in a good mood."

I wiped a drizzle of raspberry jelly off the corner of my lip. "And if Chase is grouchy, Parker will be even grouchier. I swear they like to one up each other when they are in a bad mood. I should probably finish this donut for fortification."

"Good idea." Myrna laughed as she walked back to her desk.

Parker's door swung open just as I pushed the last large bites of donut into my mouth. My cheeks were full and bloated with sugary dough and jelly when Chase came marching out of the office. As often as Myrna liked to embellish her descriptions, it seemed she had been spot on about Chase's mood. A brisk, chilly air followed him as he swept back to his desk and sat down hard enough to move his desk forward an inch.

My best bet was to allow him to finish his tantrum on his own. Chase and I had not grown close or formed much of a friendship and I saw no reason to change that now. He was one of those strikingly handsome, immaculately dressed and groomed men who easily attracted women or at least women who liked that polished style. I preferred someone with a little less attention to appearance and more attention to charisma.

"Can't believe I have to spend my time interviewing wack-adoodle ghost chasers," he muttered loudly enough to make sure I heard him.

I contemplated ignoring his complaint but the phrase ghost chasers caught my attention. I spun my chair back to face his desk. He was wearing a new designer sweater over a blue collared shirt and his hair had enough product to give it a glassy shine.

"Did you say ghost chasers?" I barely got the question out when Parker bellowed my name.

"Taylor, why are you sitting at your desk?"

I spun back around, leaving my question still lingering in the air behind me. "Did you want to see me, Mr. Seymour?"

His deep glower caused his heavy moustache to rock back and forth under his nose.

"Right," I said and grabbed a notepad. "Of course you want to see me." I hopped up from the desk and headed toward his office.

"Sunni would do a much better job with those paranormal society people. She likes those kinds of odd ball assignments,"

Chase added, completely ignoring that Parker's glower grew more menacing with each word.

I scowled back at Chase to let him know he'd just erased the check in the bonus column he'd earned from buying donuts.

I turned back to Parker. "If it's an article about the Applegate Paranormal Preservation Society, I wouldn't mind taking that story on. In fact, coincidentally enough—" I started but was cut abruptly off by Parker.

"You know something, Evans. You're right," Parker said sharply enough to assure all of us that he was absolutely not agreeing with Chase. "We'll give the paranormal society story to Taylor. You'll probably just mess it up anyhow. And frankly it's too important of a story. There's a massive convention of ghost hunters every October and they are considering holding it here in Firefly Junction. It would be a huge boost to business in the area." Parker pointed his thick finger at me. "So make sure you do a good job. Make it flattering. Pretend you believe in ghosts if you have to."

I pressed my knuckle to my mouth to silence a snicker. "Uh, I think I can be open-minded when it comes to the spirit world."

"That's right," Parker grunted. "You're good friends with that flighty, extravagant psychic, Raine or Storm or whatever her name is." He was truly in a terrible mood but I needed to stand up for my friend.

"Raine is neither flighty nor extravagant. People have a great deal of respect for her talents." I changed course before I got myself into trouble. "I'm happy to do the article on the Applegate Society. It just so happens, the Cider Ridge Inn is one of their stops this week."

Chase blew an immature sound from his mouth. "Guess they're planning to have a chat with the Cider Ridge ghost. Love to hear how that goes," he sniped.

"You won't have time to hear," Parker said. "There's a labor dispute at the sanitation department. A whole lot of stink in the air, literally and metaphorically. That'll be just up your alley, Evans. Head over there now. The two sides are about to meet to hash out a contract."

I peered back at Chase. His mouth opened into an O. "Wait, is that all you have? I don't want that assignment. I'll take those ghost whisperers instead. At least they'll be good for a laugh."

"Too late," Parker barked. "My mind's made up. Now go out there and write me something about garbage that isn't your usual garbage." With that, he slipped back into his office and snapped the door shut.

CHAPTER 4

*I*t seemed my day was filled with requests to make sure the Applegate Paranormal Preservation Society, better known as APPS, felt welcome and inspired by our small town. Considering I'd only just heard of the society an hour earlier, they had inadvertently become the full focus of my day. I was grateful that I'd said yes to Lana's request. It would be much easier to interview the group while they were staying right inside my house.

House, such a strong, non-ambiguous word, only the inn was still far from being a proper home. While I was certain the visitors looked forward to the ambience and shadowy gloom my ramshackle inn had to offer, I had to make sure they were comfortable and safe. The formal dining room had been mostly restored, subfloors tightened up and plaster holes filled. Wallpaper, painting and fixtures had been put on indefinite hold since the electricity project became a priority but the cavernous room would make a great meeting place. Lana would no doubt add her own creative flare to make the group feel pampered and pleased during their brief stay.

Myrna came out from the back room with a stack of sticky notes. She balanced them like a tottering tower on one hand while she knocked on Parker's door with the other.

"Come in," he barked.

His harsh tone never affected Myrna. She handled his sour moods better than anyone. The man loved to write everything on sticky notes. His desk and computer were decorated with dozens of them. A rainbow colored stack of sticky notes was sure to improve his mood. Chase had thundered out of the office a few minutes after Parker had ordered him to cover the labor dispute at the sanitation department. Myrna waved Chase out with an enthusiastic grin. She had cleverly joked that the two of us were sandwiched between two stale pieces of bread with both men in a foul mood. The other slice of stale bread had been holed up in his office all morning.

My fingers hovered over my keyboard. I couldn't do much for my story until the group arrived in town but I could use the time to do a little research about APPS. I typed in the very long name of the group and was rewarded with numerous entries.

The Paranormal Preservation Society was founded in 1960 by Martin Applegate. A few grainy pictures showed a young man with thick wavy hair and round John Lennon style glasses standing in front of a Volkswagen bus with the letters APPS painted along the side. On further reading, I discovered that his son, Kenneth Applegate born in 1964, joined him on his cross country ghost adventures. A side note mentioned that Martin Applegate had been heir to a sizable fortune but he had lived frugally, interested more in his ghostly pursuits than living the life of a well-to-do heir. Martin kept a large journal of all his travels to spirit filled places and Kenneth had it compiled into a memoir titled, *Haunted Applegate Adventures*. It was published three years ago and the reviews were glowing.

The next entry focused more on current day adventures of the

APPS group. According to a press release by the book publisher, Martin Applegate died just two years before the book's release. Kenneth Applegate had taken over the society five years before his father's death. I skimmed various articles and from the samples I read, Kenneth Applegate took the paranormal preservation thing quite seriously. "Ghosts should not be considered aberrations or ghouls or incorporeal nuisances," Kenneth wrote in a book fore-word for another writer.

"Well . . ." I tilted my head from side to side. "You haven't met mine," I muttered to myself.

Myrna popped quickly out of Parker's office. Her head shake caused a strand of hair to fall from her bun. "Thought those sticky notes would do the trick." She plopped into her chair. "Stay clear of him today. He thinks he's getting the flu and is using that as his excuse to be a grizzly bear." She rolled her eyes. "He's always on the cusp of some illness only nothing ever comes of it." In that, Myrna was not exaggerating. Parker Seymour was a textbook hypochondriac.

I continued reading Mr. Applegate's statement. "Ghosts are the free spirits that most of us strive to be. They should be respected, observed and celebrated."

I sat back and stared at the screen. "The man is positively enamored with ghosts." Was I making a mistake allowing him into the inn? What if he had a sixth sense strong enough to detect Edward's presence? Now that my skeptic days were one tall roguish Englishman behind me, it was much easier for me to believe that there were people who could ferret out disquieted spirits. Raine was certain I was living with a ghost but she had never heard or seen him. No one heard or saw Edward unless he chose to reveal himself. That thought relaxed me some.

I went back to my research. Angela Applegate, the younger sister of Kenneth, was the treasurer and secretary of the society. Their membership fluctuated yearly but the board was made up of five people, including the Applegate siblings. I clicked on the book where Kenneth had written the foreword. It was titled *Those Living Among Us* a rather cryptic title for what the publisher declared as the "first and foremost handbook on paranormal detection and study".

The author was Jamie Nielsen, a name that looked familiar. I glanced back at the article listing the board members of APPS. Jamie Nielsen was on the board. It seemed I would have two published authors and specter experts milling about the inn tomorrow night. Before leaving the bookstore page for Nielsen's book, another familiar name caught my eye. Kenneth Applegate had left a review for Nielsen's book and it was far from glowing. He'd given it a one star and called it a myriad of falsehoods and conjecture based on flimsy facts. Unfortunately for Nielsen, Applegate's review was front and center on the book's page. It seemed especially odd that someone would first agree to write a foreword for another author's book and then disparage the book badly in a review. It could only be assumed that the two men were well acquainted given that Nielsen was a member of the board for the society.

Myrna's intercom buzzed and Parker's deep voice grumbled through it. "Myrna, can you bring me that orange juice in the refrigerator? I'm feeling sicker by the minute. Oh, and grab a few of those donuts on the way."

Myrna sighed. "How sick can he be if he's got an appetite for donuts?" she asked me. Unfortunately, I wasn't the only person to hear the question.

"What's that?" Parker snapped through the intercom.

Myrna's face blanched but only for a second. She knew Parker couldn't run the newspaper office without her. "Darn button is always sticking." She pressed it to speak. "Nothing, Mr. Seymour," she said sweetly. "I was just telling Sunni that I put aside your favorites, maple bar and crumb donut holes."

I flinched when she said my name because I knew it would remind him that I was still sitting out in the office.

"Sunni is still out there?" he growled. I knew him too well already.

Myrna pulled her mouth tight and gave me an apologetic shrug.

"Why isn't she out talking to those ghost hunters? Advertisers will flock to the paper if Firefly Junction hosts that convention."

"I'm doing research right now, Mr. Seymour," I called loudly across the room. "The society isn't getting to town until tomorrow," I continued.

"Taylor!" he shouted, causing both Myrna and me to flinch. "Why are you yelling across the room when my office is twenty feet away?"

Myrna gave me a second shrug as she mouthed the word 'sorry'.

I grabbed my notebook and walked to his office. I knocked once before opening the door.

Parker lifted his big hand to stop me from entering. "Don't come near. I'm contagious or you might be contagious. Or we might both be contagious. Either way, my immune system has been compromised by the stressful morning. Evans is to blame for that. What is it you need, Taylor?"

I stood in the doorway, not daring to take a step inside. "You told me not to shout across the room so I came to the office."

He waved me out. "I didn't call you to the office. I was just asking why you were shouting. Now go get that interview and make sure that screwy bunch of ghost chasers sound unscrewy.

CHAPTER 5

*R*aine pushed up her long, flowing sleeves as she sat on the bench across from me. The sleeves slid right back down to her ring covered fingers.

"Hope you don't mind if we eat outside," I said as I handed her the menu. "I can't get enough of the fall breeze. And the pretty colors. Such a relief after a sticky summer." The tall tulip poplars circling Layers, our favorite lunch spot, had just begun to slip into the glorious butter yellow glow of autumn. It was my first fall in Firefly Junction and I was waiting anxiously for all the trees to show off their fiery orange and red plumage, something I sadly missed when I worked in the city where the only sign of fall was the occasional sweater and scarf sale at the local department store.

"I suppose city slickers like yourself are always awestruck by fall colors but after a few years of raking leaves just to find the front lawn, the whole thing sort of loses its charm." Raine put down the menu. "I think it's a Vincent Price sort of day, a patty melt with lots of grilled onions."

"I was thinking something light and fresh like the Lucille Ball. I love the pickled vegetables Ballard puts on the hummus."

Raine took her glasses off and began to clean them with the ends of her shirt. She looked unusually dour.

I reached for my glass of water. "You look sort of glum and I'm an expert at detecting glum today because the newspaper office was ripe with it."

"It's that silly Applegate group that's coming to town. Paranormal preservers or whatever they consider themselves."

"Ah, Lana told you about the visit?"

Raine put her glasses back on and blinked behind the thick lenses to make sure she'd erased all the smears. "She told me. I'm heading over to Lana's after lunch to help her plan a menu for their stay at the Cider Ridge Inn. I can't believe she talked you into hosting them."

I raised a brow. "You can't? Seriously? We're talking about the woman who could talk a grizzly bear out of a pot of honey with hardly a wink and a nod."

"True. And you're kind of a pushover."

"Thanks, *friend.*"

"You're right. Sorry. I shouldn't have brought my bad mood to lunch." She lifted her hands and shook them like she was drying them. Her bracelets did a hoola-hoop style dance around her thin wrists. "There. All the bad juju is gone." She pushed the corners of her lips up and held a smile. "See, the ever-charming and happy Raine is back."

Ballard, the owner of Layers, came out with her order pad. "Have you two decided on lunch?" Ballard was the culinary and marketing genius behind Layers. It was the most popular eating spot in town.

Raine grabbed the menu. "I was in a terrible mood a few minutes ago and I was certain the Vincent Price was the way to go but I'm feeling less wretched so I'm going to pick something else. Start with Sunni. It'll only take me a second to decide."

"I'll have the Lucille Ball with an extra scoop of pickled veggies."

"You know what, me too." Raine handed Ballard the menu.

Ballard tucked her pencil behind her ear. "Lana came in here earlier for a breakfast sandwich. She said you were hosting the Applegate Paranormal Preservation Society this week."

"My sister can spread news faster than melted butter. Yep, they are spending tomorrow night at the inn, hoping to make contact with the infamous Cider Ridge ghost."

Raine scoffed loudly. "Good luck with that. Those frauds couldn't conjure smoke from a blazing hearth."

Something told me my lunch partner was going to switch back to a Vincent Price. Or possibly even a Bela Lugosi, liver pate on pumpernickel.

"Well, no pressure, Sunni," Ballard continued unabated by Raine's negative comment, "but it sure would be sweet if that big paranormal convention happened here in Firefly Junction. Lots of business."

"So I've heard from my sister, my boss and now you. But no pressure. All I can do is make sure no one falls through a broken floorboard or gets a splinter from the door casings. My place is not exactly homey and inviting yet. And I have no control over the ghost in my house."

Both women looked at me.

"I mean if there is a ghost. I certainly wouldn't know it because as I said, I have no control over the supposed spirits living in the inn. Can I get a bag of chips too," I added for a less than subtle topic change.

"Yes, coming right up." Ballard was just about to spin around and head inside but something behind me caught her eye. Whatever it was, it made that same eye twinkle with admiration. Raine's eyes sparkled too.

I was just about to look back over my shoulder when Raine kicked my shoe. "Don't look. It's too obvious."

"Uh, I think the pair of you are already making it obvious." I had a vague idea of just who might be walking up behind me. I no longer needed to guess.

"Detective Jackson," Ballard said with a much more frilly tone than I had ever heard. "I've got your sandwich ready. I'll go fill your soda."

"Great. Thanks, Ballard."

It had been a few weeks since I'd seen or spoken to Detective Brady Jackson. My reaction to the sound of his voice was disconcerting. I would have preferred no reaction so I could more easily convince myself that the incredibly tall and good looking detective was just an acquaintance. But acquaintances don't normally make your heart race.

A large shadow fell over the table. I peered up at Jackson. He pushed his sunglasses up into his unruly hair. Although I had to admit it seemed as if he'd put a few more seconds into his grooming session this morning to tame his lion's mane. He hadn't vanquished the windswept look that he wore so well.

I smiled up at him. "Detective Jackson," I said cheerily. "Nice to see you."

"Good to see you too, Miss Taylor."

"Vincent Price," Raine said suddenly. She slapped the table. "I should always go with my first choice. Isn't that what they told us to do on tests?" She swung her black boots around from the bench. "I'll be right back. I need to go tell Ballard to change my order." My best friend knew I was somewhat smitten with Detective Jackson so it was entirely possible she hadn't really changed her mind back to Vincent Price. Either way, she was off in a flurry of colorful cotton.

Jackson took a seat on the bench across from me. His amber eyes looked pale in the afternoon sunlight drizzling through the poplars. He rested his muscular forearms along the edge of the table. The blue shirt he was wearing went nicely with his golden skin tone. "And what have you been up to my busy little bluebird? Guess the news business is slow when murders are scarce."

I nodded. "I was just thinking that we needed a good throat slashing or poisoning to liven things up around here."

He smiled at my dark sarcasm. "I've missed ya, Bluebird. Guess you're busy with the inn."

"Yes and work and my sisters and everything else that keeps falling onto my plate. I've been asked to host the Applegate Paranormal Preservation Society for a night at my haunted inn."

He laughed. "That is a long sounding name for a silly sounding society. How do they preserve people who are already dead?"

I pointed at him. "You see. That's what I thought at first until my sister explained that their goal is to make sure lingering spirits live a full—" I tapped my chin. "What was that word? Oh yes, a full un-life."

His laugh was deep and rich. Naturally. "That sounds like a lot of fun." Raine stepped outside and she looked around as if she was trying to find another excuse to leave Jackson and me alone at the table.

"Raine, here's your spot," Jackson said. He threw his long leg over the bench. "Sunni and I were just catching up." He waved to the empty bench with a flourish. Raine fiddled with her glasses as she sashayed past him to sit.

"Catch you two later." He nodded specifically at me. "And stay out of trouble."

The giggle spurting from Raine's lips sounded nothing like her real laugh. "We'll try."

Both Raine and I let our gazes linger overlong on Detective

Jackson as he strolled to the restaurant door and disappeared inside.

Raine flipped forward to face me. "Well, how was it?"

"How was what? Our ten second conversation? Just fine. We talked about throats being slashed or wrung. It was all quite romantic."

She huffed in frustration. "You've got to work on your flirting, my friend. And besides I couldn't think of any other good excuse to stay inside longer." She tapped the side of her head. "The bathroom, duh. Oh well probably just as well. You would have just gone on to talk about murders and mayhem." She took a sip of water. "So APPS will be at the inn tomorrow night? I should drop by and pay them a visit. The only true talent in that group is Jamie Nielsen. He wrote a great book called—"

"*Those Living Among Us*," I interjected.

"Yes. Have you read it?"

I tilted my head. "What do you think?"

"You should read it. It might just make you a believer."

"Who's to say I'm not a believer? I just don't have to waste time reading books by ghost experts when I hang out with a top of the line spirit medium."

Raine blushed at my compliment. "I suppose you're right." She sighed. "Now if I could just make contact with that darn elusive Cider Ridge Inn ghost."

"I'm sure he's around, Raine. Maybe he just doesn't like to make himself too obvious." I picked up my water.

"That's it." She snapped her fingers. "He's shy. Why didn't I think of that before. I just need to read up on how to get a shy ghost to reveal itself."

I smiled inwardly at the notion of Edward, the most opinionated, outspoken arrogant apparition ever to grace the spirit world being too shy.

CHAPTER 6

*E*verything was wonderful about the transition to autumn except that there were less hours of daylight. But a setting sun didn't stop me from making the short trek to my sister Emily's house. I would be rewarded for my dusk adventure with a basket of the first apples of the year and goat snuffles. Snuffles wasn't a technically accurate word for the sweet kisses from Emily's goats, Tinkerbell and Cuddlebug but it was the best term I could come up with for warm fuzzy snouts pushing eagerly against my skin.

With the sun close to setting, the girls, as I called them, would be safely tucked away in the barn, out of view of nighttime predators. Delicious aromas wafted through Emily's kitchen window and mingled with the earthy odors of the farm. Excluding the unique smell hovering around the chicken yard. Emily's feathery brood had a *perfume* all their own.

I spotted Emily's white blonde hair in the kitchen window. She was washing something in the kitchen sink. She tapped the window and waved at me as I crossed the yard with Newman and

Redford in tow. I pointed toward the barn and pantomimed hugging myself to let her know I needed a goat cuddle before I came inside.

She understood me perfectly and nodded. The dogs, however, had no desire to see goats or anything else except whatever treat Emily had in her dog cookie jar.

As I rounded the barn door, I stopped just short of smacking into Nick, my brother-in-law. He had switched his summer caps and straw cowboy hat out for a dark green knitted beanie.

"Hey, Sunni. Coming to get some apples? They're kind of small but really crisp. Lana took a bunch to make apple pie."

"Did she? Then I hope she's making me a pie. I'm doing her a big favor. She already seduced me with her date nut bars but this favor is big enough to earn a pie too."

Nick hung up the mucking rake on the hook. "Yeah, she told us about the paranormal group having a slumber party at the inn. She's talked Emi into baking her blackberry hand pies for the event. She's inside right now making them. Are you coming inside?"

"Right after I see my two angels, Tinkerbell and Cuddlebug."

"Angels"—He laughed dryly—"That's a good one. Emi hung one of her rugs out to dry on the laundry line and Cuddlebug ate all the tassels."

I stifled a laugh. "Did she at least chew them all to the same length?"

"She didn't need to. By the time Emi caught her all the tassels were gone. I'll see you inside."

I grabbed a handful of hay and walked to Butterscotch's stall. The Belgian mare walked to the door to nibble the hay. "They've got you locked in early. I guess that's why I didn't find you outside the inn today." I patted her and headed down to the goat pen.

Cuddlebug was knelt down in a soft spot on her straw bed. She bleated quietly but was too lazy to get up and greet me. Tinkerbell, on the other hand, trotted over and stood up on her back legs, so I could scratch her head. "You two are already bedded down for the night. Auntie will have to make the walk over here earlier or we're never going to have time to play." I rubbed Tink's soft gray ears, said good night to all the animals and headed toward the farmhouse. Emily and Nick's two-story century old farmhouse with its gabled roofs, brick chimneys and peeling red paint looked picture perfect in its grassy setting with the colorful Smoky Mountains as its backdrop.

I headed up the back steps and into Emily's heavenly smelling kitchen. Two trays of rectangular hand pies were cooling on racks on the table.

Nick was already eating his pie, dipping it in vanilla ice cream before each bite.

"Yum, I want mine with ice cream too." I walked to the cupboard and took down a bowl.

Emily brought me the tub of ice cream and a spoon. "I hear Lana talked you into a slumber party with ghost hunters."

I filled the bowl with a healthy scoop of ice cream. Emily handed me a warm blackberry pie.

"I don't know if you can refer to Lana's coercion techniques as talking into but she convinced me it will be good for the town. As long as they have a good time and enjoy their stay. And I'm supposed to flatter them with an interview in the *Junction Times*. It feels like the whole town is counting on me to make sure the ghost hunters have their convention here next month." I dipped my pie into the ice cream and closed my eyes to enjoy the bite. "Hmm, this takes away the stress of the day."

Nick was down to just ice cream. He grabbed a spoon from the caddy. "At least it's not all on your Cider Ridge ghost. Lana said they were also making a stop at the Dandelion Inn in Birch Highlands. I hear that ghost is much more active than your ghost."

I wiped my mouth with a napkin. "My ghost? Anyhow they can

conjure and summon and turn on all their ghost machines, my ghost is not going to make an appearance." (With any luck.)

"Then Lauren Grace will just have to flow out of the Dandelion walls in her shimmering white dress and long silk hair." Nick noticed he'd gotten both Emily's and my attention with his description.

He shrugged. "I didn't make that up. There's a portrait of Lauren Grace, the original owner of the Dandelion Inn hanging over the mantel in the dining room. She's wearing a long gauzy dress or night rail or something. Apparently she was quite the stunner back in the day and when she was alive, of course. People have spotted her on the landing of the staircase in that same white dress. Supposedly she died when she fell down the steps."

I finished the pie and was angry at myself for eating it so fast. "It sounds like the portrait helps people imagine a woman in a long white dress. If she were wearing a yellow polka dotted pair of pants in the portrait, I'll bet less people would see her floating around."

Emily piled the pies into a container. "Now that you mention it, Sunni, I can't say I've ever seen a ghost in a movie or picture wearing yellow polka dot pants. You might be onto something. That portrait puts the image in people's heads and then it's much easier to conjure up Lauren Grace's spirit."

Nick licked the last drop of ice cream off his spoon. "Too bad there isn't some portrait of that poor guy who took the bullet in the duel on your front yard. Maybe it would be easier for people to see him."

Just what Edward needs, a portrait of himself to admire. "You might be right about that, Nick. Hopefully the group won't be too disappointed in the lack of paranormal activity in the Cider Ridge Inn."

CHAPTER 7

The lights in the bathroom flickered on and off as I finished my makeup. Thankfully, Edward's Victorian era propriety kept him from lingering anywhere near my *private rooms* as he termed them. My bedroom and bathroom were off limits just like the world past my front porch. Only he'd voluntarily created the border on this side of the house. The front yard and everything beyond it were off limits because his spirit was confined to the house where he died. I supposed it was a good thing that unhappy haunts weren't allowed to wander the earth freely. The world would be a chaotic mess, even more so than it was without disenchanted souls causing havoc.

The lights went off just as I finished my mascara. My windowless bathroom was drowned in darkness. I had to feel for the doorknob. My fingers wrapped around it just as the lights flashed back on. They flickered for a few seconds before going off again.

I left the bathroom and headed to the cellar door in the kitchen. Tom Fielding's work lights must have been running on their own battery pack. I shielded my eyes from the harsh glow bursting up the basement stairs. "Tom, the lights are out. I'm still getting ready for work. Haven't made my coffee yet."

His giant head peered around the corner where the antiquated fuse box was located. "Are you sure? I haven't turned off the electricity yet."

I turned back and glanced to the clock on the stove. "Yes, it's off."

Tom scratched his wide chin. "Hmm, not sure what's happening but then these old houses are such a wiring mess it could have nothing to do with my work. I'll see what I can find out."

"Thanks."

"The man is an imbecile," Edward scoffed behind me. I shut the cellar door, even though there was no way Tom could have heard the comment.

"I'm sure it's something that can easily be fixed. It has to be. I'm hosting visitors tonight, my first at the Cider Ridge Inn."

"I can tell you that the light fixtures buzzed, fizzled, popped and did everything but emit light yesterday while you were out of the house. I think you can expect to give your visitors quite the show this evening." Edward swept up Newman's ball. The dog sat straight up from his morning nap as if someone had flipped on his switch. Edward popped the ball up into the air and Newman caught it snugly between his teeth.

"Don't play catch with him right now. I'm late for work and there is no coffee and I'm already tense about tonight." I pulled the coffee carafe out from the machine and shook it to see if there was enough for a cold cup. "Darn it. There's not enough coffee here for a mouse. I'm going to have to stop by the coffee shop." I took a step and the tennis ball whizzed past my head and bounced off the wall before shooting back toward Newman.

I turned a fiery gaze on Edward. He shrugged his vaporous shoulders. "Sorry it slipped."

"It slipped? Balls don't generally fly like missiles when they've slipped. Please, Edward. Can't you find someplace else to be right now? I'm not in the mood for your antics."

"You are very disagreeable this morning." He floated up to his favorite perch on the kitchen hearth.

"Guilty as charged and yet I plan to stay disagreeable." The pressure suddenly placed on me by my sister and my editor had really pushed me out of the wrong side of the bed. Tom, in the center of it all, fudging with the electricity only made things worse.

The lights turned back on. I waited a moment to see if they had stabilized. It seemed they had. I quickly filled the coffee maker and dumped a good scoop of medium roast into the basket. I was going to need an extra kick today. I pushed the on button and the pot whispered its comforting hissing sound to let me know in a few minutes I'd be sipping a hot, rich cup of Joe.

The gentle sigh of all the appliances turning off followed. The green brewing light went off and I was back to square one. "Oh, come on. Not today."

Car doors and voices took me to the front window. Raine and Lana were deep in conversation, arms loaded with boxes. "Of course. And now my sister shows up to revamp the dining room for the guests." I zipped past Edward who was watching my hectic morning from his perch.

I swung open the front door. "Please tell me there's a fresh pot of coffee in one of those boxes."

Lana carried her box up the step. "I could tell you there is but I'd be lying."

Raine grinned as she trudged past with her box. "Sorry no coffee here either. Just linens, silverware and dishes."

"Could you grab the baskets from the truck, Sunni?" Lana called as she was halfway to the dining room.

"Sure, I've got nothing better to do this morning," I muttered as I walked out to Lana's truck. Lana had filled individual baskets with snacks, pens, notepads, and mini flashlights. She'd hand-painted names on each flashlight. I grabbed two of the baskets and carried them into the house.

Lana was standing in the center of my unfinished dining room mind mapping the arrangement of chairs and air mattresses. She pointed to the corner of the room for me to set down the baskets. Her hands settled on her hips as she stared up at the bare wires curling down from the ceiling. "I forgot you don't have a chandelier in here yet. There's plenty of light now through the windows but I'll need to bring over some lamps to set up around the room."

"Might be a lot of trouble for nothing." I lowered the baskets to the unfinished hardwood floors. "The electricity is being fickle this morning. Hence my impassioned plea for coffee."

Lana's lip curled. "Uh oh, Sunni without coffee can make for a bad morning. I could go back to the farm and make you a pot."

"No, I'll get some on the way to work. Tom Fielding is here working on the electricity. Hopefully he'll figure out why the lights are flickering on and off this morning. Guess those cute personal flashlights will come in handy."

Edward's constant need to be entertained by earthly humans brought him to the dining room. I scowled quickly at him which only made his image solidify more. Raine stomped right past him with two more baskets. She stumbled forward and nearly dropped the goodies. I froze to the spot as she swished her head back and forth looking for something. "Did you guys feel that?"

"Feel what?" Lana asked.

"It felt like someone brushed my arm with cold air."

I snuck a questioning look at Edward. He returned a sheepish smile. Ever since Raine had conducted a séance in the house to summon Edward, he'd found great entertainment in teasing her.

Raine wriggled once as if to get rid of a creeping sensation. "APPS certainly picked the right place for their visit. It seems the air is thick with paranormal activity today. Too bad they are mostly a bunch of amateurs. They'll probably miss every subtlety."

"Actually," Lana said, "flickering lights are perfect. Ghosts are always doing stuff like that."

Edward laughed dryly. "What nonsense. Why on earth would ghosts do something as mundane as turning lights on and off? Maybe I should pull on a bed sheet and yell boo as well."

I stomped my foot lightly and glowered at him to be quiet.

"Woo, sis, you need to go get that coffee. You're scowling like the Grinch this morning. Just leave all this to Raine and me and don't worry about a thing. I'm sure the visitors will hear plenty of creaks and moans in this old place, enough to keep their overactive imaginations chattering for months."

Raine cleared her throat loudly to show her displeasure at Lana's comment. "The cold touch on my arm had nothing to do with my imagination. It happened. There is a ghost in this house sure as there is a nose on my face."

Lana put up her hand to stop Raine's lecture. "Yes, you're right. But you have to understand, Raine, people like Sunni and me, who have no psychic ability, no connection to the afterworld, have a hard time believing. It's easy to be a skeptic when you can't hear or feel or sense paranormal events. So you have to give us a break."

I was just disgruntled enough from my morning to feel defensive. "Don't lump me into your skeptic world, Lana. I sense things plenty in this house. Sometimes I'm even irritated by all of it." I raised a brow at Edward. He lifted his in return just before vanishing.

Lana appeared somewhat stunned at my confession. She laughed dryly. "Are you saying you've seen ghosts in the house?"

Raine's eyes widened as she waited breathlessly for my response. If there was anyone in the world I wanted to reveal my secret to, it was Raine. But I'd made a promise to Edward. Besides it was entirely up to him. He decided who could hear and see him and at the moment that club was small, namely myself and two border collies who weren't very discerning about the company they kept.

"I'm not saying I've seen an actual ghost," I said.

Lana's expression and condescending nod came straight out of the big sister's handbook on putting silly little sisters in their place.

"I just prefer to keep a more open mind," I said, adding in a little sister's 'so there' chin lift. It had about as much effect as it did back when I was ten.

"See, Sunni is a true friend," Raine quipped. "Now where do I put the air mattresses?"

"I'm out of here," I said. "Must. Have. Coffee." I waved on my way out the door.

CHAPTER 8

A heavy, aroma-filled mist hovered around those in line at the coffee shop. The woman in front of me had apparently pulled the short straw, giving her the task of buying coffee for the entire office. And what a picky, spoiled bunch of coffee drinkers they were. Half a squirt of this, only low fat on that, almond milk only, a dollop of nonfat whipping cream. The comical concept of nonfat whipping cream gave me my first laugh of the morning. The barista, a tiny woman who moved like a ninja around the kitchen, gave the woman with the long picky list a piece of her mind, letting her know next time they needed to order in advance of the pickup. I kept my hands straight down at my sides to avoid breaking into a round of applause for the barista.

I reached the counter and inadvertently braced my hands against it as if I had just stumbled in from a trek across the desert and was one step away from dying of thirst. "A grande coffee of the day. As rich and black as you've got. In fact if you leave out the water I'm all right with that."

The young girl at the register peered up in question.

"No, I'm kidding. Water is fine. Makes it easier to sip through that little slit in the top."

She laughed weakly, apparently not finding my humor all that humorous. She spun around and I stared at the coffee as it cascaded into the cup.

"Should I leave room for cream?" she asked.

"Fill it so it's seeping out the top."

"Someone needs their coffee fix this morning." Even with my senses sluggish from lack of caffeine, I could easily recognize the deep voice behind me. Once my fingers were wrapped securely around my coffee cup, I turned around.

Detective Jackson was standing fresh faced and ready to start his day with shiny badge on belt, dark sunglasses sitting on his head and a very pretty redhead at his side. Her blue pencil skirt, blouse and high heeled shoes made it clear she wasn't his new partner.

The hello stuck in my throat. The morning had started badly. There was certainly no reason for my fortunes to change wind at this point. Seeing him with a lovely woman was the perfectly spectacular finale. And my reaction to seeing him with another woman assured me that I was way too enamored with the man. I needed to squelch my apparent crush and fast. After devoting many good years to a man who in the end opted for someone he considered more suited to his doctor lifestyle, the last thing I needed was to fall for a man who no doubt had a phone contact list filled with women's names.

"You're clutching that coffee like it might try and run away from you," he quipped. I was thankful he left off the Bluebird nickname. But I wasn't sure if that was because it spared me odd looks from his date or if because I was fond of it. I was really in a muddle this morning.

I took a sip to clear my head. It didn't help as much as I hoped. "Yes." I lifted the cup. "Heaven help the individual who tries to come between me and my cup of medium roast. I don't want to block the line. It was nice seeing you." The redhead was too busy deciding on her coffee choice to pay me much mind which was fine by me.

I nodded to Jackson and sidled through the other customers and out the door.

I was only a few feet from the jeep when I heard the nickname I'd been both fretting and wanting to hear.

"Hey, Bluebird, wait a second."

I closed my eyes before turning around to gather my wits. I was relieved to see he was alone as he closed the gap quickly between us with his long strides. "Are you all right? You don't seem yourself."

For some reason, his question unexpectedly released the stopper. "Myself? Not quite. I've got a group of complete strangers coming to stay in my house, a house that is hardly fit for rats and mice let alone out of town visitors. The boss is telling me to write a glowing story about the same people, group of ghost chasers, so that they bring their big convention to town next month. My sister is turning the screws on me for the same reason." I put up two fingers. "So that's two people I'll disappoint if the Paranormal Preservation Society isn't pleased with their stay or their article." The rant, newly fueled by the three gulps of coffee I had on the way to the jeep, kept flowing. "Then of course I have to worry that my ghost doesn't screw things up with his usual selfishness." I blinked up at him and tried to assess whether or not he heard the last detail in my flurry of angry declarations.

His faintly cocky smile made the lines next to his mouth crease. "Did you just say you had a selfish ghost?"

My heart paddled around my chest for a second while I constructed a response. "What? No. Did I say that?" (It was the best I could do standing with those amber eyes gazing down at me.)

"You did. You said that you had to worry about your ghost screwing things up because he was selfish."

I laughed and took a loud sip of coffee. I swallowed dramatically. "Do you see what happens to me when I don't have coffee? Which I didn't have because the electrician is working on rewiring the inn and I had no electricity this morning." It was a pathetic topic change but it seemed to work.

"Hey, Bluebird, maybe you're taking on too much. Why don't you let your sister host the group? Doesn't she have a big party barn?"

"See, why didn't I think of that?" I was still so flustered by the reality that I'd talked openly about Edward that I forgot myself and tapped his chest. He stared down at the place on his shirt for a second and then lifted his gaze to me.

"I suppose it's because her barn isn't prone to selfish screwy ghosts," he said.

I nodded. "Oh yeah that's right. They are staying at the inn because it's on some important list of haunted homes in America."

He smiled. "Is that right? That's pretty cool."

"I suppose it's cool as long as I don't have a parade of inn visitors marching through with their equipment and recorders."

He rubbed his chin. "Guess that would be a problem." There was just enough stubble on it to make me wonder if he'd spent the night somewhere other than his own home. I pushed the thought from my head. I didn't need any other aggravation this morning.

"Brady," a voice called from the coffee shop door. It was the redhead. "I've found a table."

"Be right there," he called.

I wouldn't allow myself to sink in disappointment. A man like Brady Jackson would be far more trouble than he was worth. He turned back to me and a perfectly timed breeze pushed a sun-bleached strand of hair across his face and I was rethinking my earlier assessment about the balance of trouble and worth.

"I'll let you go then, Taylor. I just wanted to make sure you were all right." He flashed another smile, only this one was different. This one stole my breath for a moment. It wasn't just because it was an extraordinary smile. I'd yet to have the man flash anything but a breathtaking smile. But this one was slightly different. For some strange reason, for the briefest second, Detective Brady Jackson bore a striking resemblance to Edward Beckett.

I shook off the weird sensation. "Yes enjoy your coffee with your friend." I hurried around to the driver's side and climbed inside. I sipped my coffee and rested my head back with my eyes closed. Work could wait. I needed a few minutes alone with my soothing cup of Joe.

CHAPTER 9

I'd managed to whisk away the fretful morning. Parker had gone to a meeting with Mr. Newsom, the owner of the paper. His mood had improved since the day before but he was still carrying a large flask of orange juice and a box of zinc tablets to ward off the impending flu or cold or general illness that was apparently ready to strike at any moment. Myrna was spending the morning cold calling businesses to sell advertising slots in the paper, a task she found 'even more loathsome than mopping the kitchen floor'. I needed to look extra busy or risk having her hand me a phone list to join her.

I'd thoroughly exhausted the online information sources for the Applegate Society, or at least all the sources worthy of reading. After a good hour of research I was staring down at a mostly blank notebook. I hated to admit it but the information and articles about the so-called paranormal experts seemed like a lot of fanciful fluff. There were stories of near misses, a shift of breeze inside a cellar, someone certain a cold hand touched them and the typical unexplained orb of light in a photo, usually a photo so dark or blurry it was hard to notice anything was amiss or for that matter supernatural. And this opinion was no longer the meandering thoughts of a hearty skeptic. I now had solid, or for lack of a better term, un-solid evidence of a ghost and he was as incredible to behold as he was annoying to live with. But it seemed none of the people in the APPS group had any firm evidence or proof of the spirit world. Perhaps Raine had been correct in her opinion and they were just a group of frauds or people who had convinced themselves of extra sensory talents that none of them actually possessed. Applegate's review had mentioned that Jamie Nielson, the member who had written the supposed handbook on paranormal detection had based much of his findings on theories and flimsy facts. After seeing his picture, a tall thirty something man with dark eyes, a goatee and with the at ease style that Raine was attracted to I decided her praise might have been more due to the man's physical appearance than his psychic abilities. Of course as far as psychic abilities went, Raine had won me over to the believer's side when she'd sadly but correctly predicted someone would die after reading cards and tea for women in a bridal party. It was a prediction that nearly got her in trouble. Apparently Tarot cards and tea leaves are not a great defense when you were privy to someone's murder.

Myrna grunted as she slammed down the phone. I sat up straight and furled my brow with interest as if something other than my cluttered chaotic desktop was staring back at me. With real purpose I typed in Cider Ridge Inn and hit enter. I'd read the majority of the mostly worthless articles about the inn. It had been awhile since I'd entered the name of the inn. This time several images came up in the small box titled images for Cider Ridge Inn. The first two boxes were taken up by what appeared to be century old photos. I clicked to open them and chirped with excitement.

The elated sound caught Myrna's attention. "I guess some people get to do amusing, wonderful internet browsing while others have to call strangers and beg them for money," she snorted.

I pointed at the monitor. "I'm researching haunted houses for my article and I found my very own haunted house."

Myrna nodded half-heartedly and dialed the next number.

I scooted my chair closer and lowered my face near enough to the monitor that I could see all the fingerprints and smears on the glass. The pictures came up as items for sale in a store called Lola's Antiques. The description read 'mid-nineteenth century photo of the Cider Ridge Inn. Family playing croquet on front lawn while woman looks on from porch. For paranormal buffs, there appears to be a misty figure standing next to the woman'. The last statement made me chirp again only this one sounded like someone had stepped on my toe.

I was sitting at my desk but my heart was racing. I zoomed in as much as possible but it wasn't enough to see the grainy, faded picture clearly. My face popped up and I looked over at Myrna. She was just hanging the phone up. Her bright pink lips were pursed with annoyance.

"Myrna, do you have that magnifying glass you were using to read the small print on Parker's medicine bottle?"

"Sure do." She was pleased to step away from the dreaded cold call list. She fished through her desk drawer and got up to walk it over. I got up so quickly, my chair rolled back.

"No," I said far too abruptly, "don't trouble yourself. I'll come get it." I couldn't exactly inspect a photo with a possible image of a ghost right in front of Myrna. Especially one standing right on the porch of the inn.

I scurried across. She dropped it unceremoniously on my palm. "I could have brought it. It would have given me a break from this call list."

I put on my best sympathetic smile. "Any luck yet?"

"Nope. Businesses are always tight with their advertising money at this time of year. Of course that will change if Firefly Junction is chosen as the site of the paranormal convention next month." She winked at me. "Our top reporter will make sure that happens, then I won't have to make cold calls. They'll be calling us."

"I'm not making any promises, Myrna, but I'll do the best I can." My steps were heavier on the return trip to my desk. That dull, thudding pressure weighed down on me as I realized everyone was counting on me to flatter, cajole and praise tonight's visitors enough to win them over. For the first time ever, I wished I could expose Edward. That would certainly make Firefly Junction a shoo-in for the convention.

I sat at my chair and dallied a few seconds so Myrna's attention would be back on her phone list before I scrutinized the picture. She was also in the dallying mood as she busied herself with straightening her desk drawer, splashing on some perfume and then organizing her pens by color in the cup on her desk. With a harrumph, meant solely for me, she picked up her phone again and began dialing.

I scooted closer, lowered my face and held up the magnifying glass. The brick facade and roof on the inn looked far less shabby in the old photo, which made sense. The house would not have been all that old. The picture was of course, black and white, and most of it had faded to various shades of gray. The woman on the porch was dressed in a cumbersome hoop skirt and embroidered bodice. Short round bangs curled over her forehead. Most people in Victorian photos looked stiff and serious but this happened to be more impromptu, less staged than the usual grave and gloomy portraits of that time period. The photographer captured a moment in time at the Cider Ridge Inn which tugged at my heart strings some. The second picture was the same front view of the house but only two small children sat on the bottom step, a step I'd trod down many times. I moved the magnifying glass back to the first picture. The woman on the porch was watching her family play croquet. The entire scene in front of her was charming and serene yet her curly bangs couldn't hide the fretful crease of her brow. The photo seemed to be smeared right past the image of the woman, as if the photographer had accidentally grabbed it while it was still wet. I hovered the magnifying glass over the smear and a pair of familiar eyes stared back at me from the smudge.

I gasped in shock and dropped the glass.

Myrna was on the phone as she raised a curious brow my direction. I smiled sheepishly and picked up the glass. It took me a second to gather my courage, and then I looked at the image once more. Sure enough, Edward Beckett in waistcoat, open cravat and finely polished boots was standing on the front porch watching the children play. The woman in the picture was Mary Richards. The Richards family purchased the home from Cleveland Ross. Edward told me he'd revealed himself to Mary. Now her irritated expression made sense.

Without another thought, I pushed the buy button. A box came up that let me ask questions or make comments about the purchase. I shifted the keyboard in front of me and typed.

"Dear Lola's Antiques, I found these photos on your store's site and I'm thrilled. I am the current owner of the Cider Ridge Inn. Thank you so much for finding them. It says I can add ten dollars for overnight shipping. I will do that as I'm very anxious to see these in person. Thank you, Sunni Taylor."

A chat message popped right back. "Hello, Sunni. Thank you for your purchase. I'll get these in the mail right away. I'm excited that the pictures have found their proper home. Be sure to look them over closely. I think you'll find them very interesting. Sincerely, Lola Button."

I sat back with a smile. Maybe my secret wasn't so secret after all. It seemed Lola Button in Port Danby had seen Edward too. Of course he was far more astonishing in person than in a photo. Or could his presence be called in person? So many unanswered questions still, including the big one—why was Edward stuck in this world? Maybe the *experts* would be able to shed some light on the mystery.

CHAPTER 10

*a*fter running out of things to research on the computer, I'd needed to stretch my legs and get out of the newspaper office. Myrna's sour mood had helped me along with that idea. I decided to get a head start on the article by checking out the second inn on the group's list. Playing in numerous sports growing up had left me naturally competitive, and I found myself curious about Dandelion Inn. I'd hoped to find a dingy, out of date inn with little to offer other than the story of a ghost but was slightly disappointed. I parked the jeep in front of a pale yellow two story Victorian with a wrap-around porch and large rooster weathervane topping off one of two turrets. The windows and decorative trim were painted in a gray-blue color that contrasted perfectly with the yellow facade. Feathery yellow and green shrubs lined the front porch and white roses climbed along the white columns framing the front entrance.

Kitty Bloomfield, the owner of Dandelion Inn, had been gracious and charming on the phone when I called and introduced myself. I should have guessed that her inn would be lovely.

Suddenly, my ramshackle monstrosity with the flickering lights and broken windows seemed impossibly far from ever becoming a welcoming bed and breakfast.

I climbed the steps to the front door, painted in the same charming blue as the trim. A large wreath of green ivy and white roses hung on the tall paneled door. Two sidelights contained intricate stained glass windows depicting dandelions and butter-flies. I rang the doorbell. Even the chime was adorable. APPS was certainly going to enjoy their stay here after a night in Cider Ridge.

That thought took a good dose of steam out of my engine. I was close to turning around and trudging dejectedly back to my jeep when the front door opened. A peppery aroma swirled out from the house, followed quickly by lavender perfume.

"You must be Sunni," the woman cheered. "I'm Kitty. Welcome, welcome." Kitty Bloomfield looked to be in her mid sixties. She was a petite woman with a pile of pinkish-blonde curls on top of her head. Her white angora sweater was held together on the top by a silver clip that was shaped like a dragonfly. As she led me through the wallpaper-lined foyer, she discretely brushed her fingers along an entry table to check for dust. She paused just long enough to adjust one of the yellow sunflowers sitting in the crystal vase.

"I put on a pot of tea," Kitty half sang as I followed her through the hallway past a flight of stairs that was lined with an ornately carved oak banister. The stairwell and adjacent room, a sitting room filled with plump cozy chairs and sitting nooks were deco-rated in pink and blue wallpaper and ornate brass light fixtures. White curtains as thin as gossamer hung over a set of three windows that looked out over a neatly groomed backyard.

"Your inn is beautiful," I said as I followed her to the dining room where an antique silver tea service was laid out on a white lace tablecloth. "It's like a picture."

Kitty's smile caused her cheeks to pile up in soft, wrinkly layers. "Aren't you sweet. I did it all myself. If you need any help at all with your inn, just ask. I've got plenty of connections in the interior design world." She winked and then ran her hand along the top of the mahogany dining room chair. It was polished to a high gloss and I could just about see myself in it, but she checked her fingers for dust. It seemed she was overly attentive to cleanliness and the inn showed it. I was going to have to work on that. I tended to linger on the opposite end of the cleanliness spectrum.

I sat on the side of the dining room table that afforded me an unobstructed view of the richly carved stone mantel. A masterfully painted portrait of a woman with an ornate gilt frame was centered over the hearth. The subject of the oil painting was a beautiful woman in a long, white dress. Her long golden tresses seemed to glow and her blue eyes sparkled with life. It had to be the portrait Nick mentioned.

Kitty noticed me admiring the painting as she poured the tea. "That is the lady of the house," she said cheerily. "Miss Lauren Grace was the belle of the neighborhood. Her father had large investments in railroads, and he was excessively wealthy." She laughed. "If one can be too rich, that is. He built her this house when her first husband, Charles, died after a fall from his horse. They had only been married two months, and Lauren was very in love with him." She clucked her tongue as if the tragedy had just taken place this week. Then a smile popped up. "Sugar?" She lifted the silver dish of sugar cubes.

"No, thank you." I took the cup of tea. "So it's Lauren's spirit that haunts the inn?"

Kitty dropped two sugars into her cup. "Yes, indeed. Poor woman fell to her death right on the stairs we passed on the way to the dining room. It has been rumored that she didn't fall accidentally."

Murder mystery nerd that I was, I sat immediately forward. "So it was murder?"

Kitty drew her face long. "Well, I'm not sure about that, but supposedly there were several men vying for her attention. Jealousy can be a strong motive, especially back in those days. I'm sure you know all about that considering the Cider Ridge ghost died in a duel with a jealous husband."

"Oh, you know about my ghost?" I cleared my throat. "About the Cider Ridge ghost?"

Her smile broadened and she touched my hand. "It's all right, dear, I'm rather proprietary about my ghost as well."

A door opened and the room filled with the peppery fragrance that'd greeted me at the door. A forty something woman with short auburn hair and a yellow checked apron hurried into the room carrying a large spoon in one hand while using her free hand to hold a dish towel to keep the contents of the spoon from falling onto the rug.

Kitty coughed over her cup of tea. "Goodness, Lucy, be careful with that. I just had these rugs cleaned."

"That's why I'm carrying the towel. I wanted you to taste this gravy for the roast beef. I think it's my best yet. That bunch of ghost groupies will love it."

Kitty flicked her gaze my direction. "This is Miss Acevado, the Dandelion Inn chef. Lucy, this is Miss Taylor, a journalist from the *Junction Times* and the owner of the Cider Ridge Inn."

Lucy's brown eyes rounded. "Wow, the Cider Ridge Inn. I'm friends with Ursula Rice. She told me she and Henry are restoring the entire house for you."

I nodded. "Yes, slowly but surely." I motioned to the spoon. "Please, don't let me get in the way of a gravy taste test."

Kitty took a tiny lady-like sip of the gravy. "Hmm, very good. Delicious."

Lucy looked at her expectantly. "Delicious but . . ."

"Needs a touch more salt," Kitty added.

"There it is." Lucy winked at me. "It's never perfect until Kitty's had the last word." The chef rustled out with her apron and spoon. Just as the chef exited through one door, another door opened.

A woman about my age with her hair covered by a red bandana and wearing large rubber gloves walked into the dining room, whistling and seemingly unaware the room was occupied. She took two faltering steps. "Oh, excuse me, I didn't realize you were having tea."

Kitty looked more than a little miffed. "That's all right, Wilma. I noticed there was some dust on the rocking chairs in the library. If you could make sure to give them an extra polish today."

Wilma nodded. "Yes, right away. Just as soon as I'm done with the bedroom suites. I just needed to get a cup of coffee from the kitchen." She smiled politely and continued on through the kitchen door.

Kitty leaned forward and I found myself inside her lavender perfume cloud. "Once you open your inn, you'll find that a good staff is the number one requirement."

"I've no doubt of that."

"Your tea is getting cold." She picked up the silver pot.

"Oh, no thank you. It's fine." I sipped it and discovered she was right, but I hadn't really come for tea. In truth, I wasn't too sure of my true motives for visiting the inn, except for the obvious ones. I tended to get fidgety sitting at my computer when I didn't have anything to write. Cold calling had made Myrna grumpy and after my own morning dalliance with a sour mood, I wanted to stay clear of her. Then there was the curiosity about my competition in the hospitality business. On that front, I was both impressed and somewhat *depressed*. The Cider Ridge Inn had such a long way to go.

Kitty patted her mouth with a napkin. "I understand you'll be hosting the Applegate group tonight."

"Yes, and now that I see your wonderful inn, I'm thankful they're coming to mine first. They would be sorely disappointed if it were the other way around. I'm not even sure why they want to stay at Cider Ridge. In its present state, it is just one step above a rustic campsite."

"They are in search of supernatural ambience not luxury." There was just enough twist of her lips to amplify the sarcasm in her tone. Her thin, narrow shoulders lifted and fell. "I do wish ghost hunters would leave those of us who live with troubled spirits alone. It's hard enough having a disquieted soul lingering about without them coming in to stir things up."

I was speechless for an awkward moment, not sure how far to go with the conversation. "So, you *do* see Lauren Grace floating around the inn?" I asked, cautiously. I wasn't about to start commiserating with Kitty about Edward, but I was extremely curious if Kitty was also dealing with a very real ghost.

Kitty sat back with her cup of tea. "Oh yes, she occasionally shows up as a shadow on the stairs or a cold breeze through the dining room. Sometimes the things on my vanity have been moved around."

"Do you talk to her?"

"Constantly telling her to knock it off and go away. Just yesterday Lucy was waving her big metal spoon in the air telling Lauren to leave her pot of stew alone. Apparently Lauren turned the burner up on the stove and the stew nearly burned."

"So she shows herself to more than one person?" I asked.

My question puzzled her. "Sure. If she's feeling extra cheeky, she shows herself to the guests."

"Shows herself?"

"Well, she doesn't so much *show* herself as she moves curtains around or makes the bedroom floors creak."

"I see." My posture crumpled. I had a hundred questions, but it seemed the Dandelion Inn ghost had more to do with easily explained disturbances than actual sightings. I moved forward with one more question. "You mentioned you talk to Lauren Grace. Does she talk back to you?"

"Indeed." She grinned with satisfaction. My back straightened again. "Not in words, of course," she continued. "But in the usual ways that spirits communicate."

"Like drapes fluttering and floors creaking?" I asked.

"Yes. Like that."

I nodded and forced myself to finish the cold tea. For a brief moment, I hadn't felt quite so alone. I was certain I'd found a confidante, a comrade, someone to exchange stories with about living with an unsettled spirit. But it seemed Kitty Bloomfield's experiences were far less astonishing than mine. While it was entirely possible that the ghost of Lauren Grace was causing stove burners to turn higher and hairbrushes to be moved around, it seemed she kept herself quite hidden from view.

"Well, it's been lovely chatting with you, Kitty. And I'm so glad I have an expert I can consult when the time comes to open Cider Ridge Inn."

She walked me to the door. I took one long glance up the staircase. No sign of any woman in a white dress.

"Stop by anytime, dear. And good luck with your visitors tonight."

CHAPTER 11

*L*ana's truck was parked in front of the inn when I pulled up. If I knew my sister, she'd been working all day to create stunning accommodations for the Applegate group. Newman and Redford did not bound to the front door to greet me, which meant Lana was probably arranging food in the kitchen. The delicious mix of aromas wafting through the house assured me my guess was right.

I stopped by the dining room to see if it was ready for the guests. I hardly recognized it as the same room. Lana had covered windows with lacy fabric, and Raine had set up air mattresses with piles of sumptuous pillows and decorative quilts. Three tables had been set with elegant linens and table settings fit for a queen. Candle and floral centerpieces sat at each table. Lana had brought in some of her party chairs, and each chair had been set with a cushion and a large sash that said "Welcome APPS". I don't know why I fretted about the group being disappointed with their stay at Cider Ridge. Lana would make sure it was memorable.

Newman and Redford sat obediently in the kitchen waiting for my sister to take notice of their hungry, pleading gazes. Lana was just setting out glass mugs on the counter in front of a drink dispenser labeled apple cider. She had covered my scarred pine work table with an orange checked table cloth and every inch of the gingham fabric was covered with trays of goodies. "Glad you're home. I just received a text from Angela Applegate. They'll be here within the hour."

"That soon? I expected them tonight, after dark. Closer to the witching hour perhaps."

"Funny little sister. Here, try some goodies. That'll put you in a good mood." Lana handed me a muffin shaped tart that smelled like onion. "It's a mashed potato puff." She continued along the table. "We've got grilled squash topped with herbed ricotta, turkey and cranberry quiche bites, black bean and corn salad, Emi's hand pies, walnut cake—" She stopped at the glass bowl shaped like a pumpkin. "And of course my fall party mix. I added some dried apple this time and it's delicious. And Raine found a recipe for toasted marshmallow milk shakes, which we'll make later when we serve the pumpkin-pecan cupcakes."

The potato puff melted in my mouth like creamy butter. I held it up. "You had me at potato puff. I guess this is a really big deal getting this account, huh?"

"Yes and I know I owe you big time." Lana skirted around the table and adjusted the napkins into a fan shaped display.

"No, you don't owe me, Lana. You do plenty for me. I'm glad to help out. And I don't think Dandelion Inn has anything on the Lana Taylor transformed Cider Ridge Inn. I just hope they won't be too disappointed by the lack of paranormal activity." As if on cue, Edward materialized on the hearth. He looked frazzled and not terrible happy. After my chat with Kitty, I made a promise to myself to start helping Edward find his way out of his stuck in the middle eternity.

"Are you kidding?" Lana pulled my attention from my somber

looking ghost. "This place practically vibrates with the supernatural. Raine had to finally take a break because she was feeling on edge from all of it."

"Is that right?" I shot a questioning brow Edward's direction. He shook his head weakly in response.

Newman and Redford bolted to their feet and went racing to the front door.

"Oh my gosh, Lana, is that the group already?"

She scooted to the kitchen window. "Oh good, this way the food won't get too cold and flat. I guess my directions were clear."

I held out my arms and stared down at my black pants and sweater. "I was hoping I had time to shower and change. Do I look all right?"

"You look fine. Let's go greet them."

I shot Edward a sideways glance as I followed Lana out of the kitchen. He vanished but I was sure it wouldn't be the last time I saw him this evening.

Lana was already on the porch when I reached the entry. "Welcome to Cider Ridge Inn," she called as the group carried their duffle bags and luggage across the grass. I recognized everyone from their online photos.

Jamie Neilson led the group with just a small backpack on his shoulders. He didn't bother to help the women with their bags. He was taller than I expected. His long hair was twisted up into a man bun and he was wearing a gray flannel shirt with his jeans and Birkenstock sandals. He looked just Raine's type, but something told me he lacked charm. I could see it in the gray eyes set deep behind black rimmed glasses.

I smiled graciously at him as I hurried down the steps to help Angela Applegate, Kenneth's younger sister, with an unwieldy piece of equipment, a recording device of some sort. She had her suitcase in the other hand. I grabbed the suitcase, not wanting to be responsible for equipment.

"Thank you so much," Angela said. Her hair was dyed a severe black which made her fair skin positively transparent. Her blues eyes held a friendly glow. "Kenneth and Rex are pulling the cameras out. Where should I put this EVP recorder?"

Lana met us on the grass and took the bag from me. She motioned to the one person I didn't recognize or see in a picture. "I'll show you where to put the equipment while Sunni helps Barbara with her things."

Barbara was a fifty-something woman with curly brown hair and large green framed eye glasses. She had two suitcases, both with wheels meant for slick airport floors and not my overgrown front lawn.

"Hello, I'm Sunni. Let me take one of those bags for you."

"Thank you." She handed me the handle on one suitcase. It seemed like a lot of clothes for a few days of ghost hunting. "That one is the heaviest. It has all my notes and reference books." She stopped after a few steps. "Kenny, do you need any help? I have a free hand." She waved her pink fingernails in the air.

Kenneth waved from the back of the car before leaning into the open trunk. "We've got it." Kenneth Applegate was in his fifties. His dark hair was combed to one side, and his thick beard had flecks of gray. His gunmetal gray sweater matched his gray slacks perfectly, making it look as if he was wearing a gray coverall. He lifted several camera bags out of the trunk. The other man, a man who I recognized as Rex Thunder, mostly because of the unusual name, carried a tripod across the grass. Watching my first proper guests trudge across the lawn reminded me that I needed to get a quote for a cement path leading to the front porch. Just another expensive item on a long list of necessities.

I carried Barbara's suitcase up the steps. She stopped several times to look back at Kenneth as he carried the camera equipment toward the porch. Ridiculously, I hadn't considered the possibility that they would be taking a lot of pictures of my very un-photogenic home. Of course, since Lana plopped this on me just yesterday, I hadn't had enough time to consider much of anything.

"Oh my," Barbara said, only it wasn't the good kind of oh my, like—oh my, your new haircut is fabulous. It was more of an—oh my, this will be a long night.

Jamie, who had not offered to help with the equipment, had already done a quick, uninvited tour of the downstairs. He adjusted his glasses. "So you're the owner?"

"Yes, hello. I'm Sunni. We didn't have a chance to meet." I badly wanted to add that we missed the chance because he rudely brushed past and into the house without so much as a smile. But I needed to be on my best behavior. It seemed the entire financial state of the town depended on it.

"Jamie Nielson," he said without a handshake. Instead, he peered up at the ceiling of the hallway. "Is this place water tight?" His laugh was stiff. "I already know it's not air tight. Seems you have more holes than plaster."

"Yes, well it's a work in progress. Excuse me." I scooted past him to the dining room. Barbara had already reached the dining room. She looked more pleased than she had been in the entryway. She chose a bed near one of the windows and placed her suitcase on the ground. I dragged the other case to the same bed.

Lana helped Angela choose just the right air mattress that wouldn't be too near any drafts. Apparently, Angela caught colds easily.

Kenneth and Rex clamored in with the rest of the equipment. "Thanks for all the help, Nielson," Rex growled. Jamie ignored him as he settled back onto the pillows on a mattress and crossed his ankles.

Rex Thunder was a short, stout man tucked tightly into a corduroy jacket that reminded me of something a college professor would have worn in the sixties. It even had soft leather elbow patches and a pocket protector with pens. I could smell his aftershave and the remnants of a cigar all the way across the room.

I smiled at Barbara and was about to tell her the direction to the bathroom, but I quickly discovered that her gaze was glued to Kenneth as he set down the cameras next to his mattress.

I cleared my throat to get her attention. She turned back to me. "Kenneth is so talented with that Night Vision Video Camera," she gushed. "Why, one night, we were in a pitch dark attic in an old house that was plagued with multiple specters. One of the specters decided to shoot through the room and push the door shut. Kenneth caught it all on camera, clear as day, as if it was happening right on a movie stage."

"Really? So you could see the ghost clearly?"

"Not exactly. Although Angela was sure she saw two yellow eyes just before the door swung shut." She dropped her gaze and busied herself with the zipper on her suitcase. "He caught whole thing on tape. The door was a good six inches ajar and then *click*, it was closed." It seemed Barbara Simpson was far more interested and intrigued by Kenneth Applegate than by any lingering spirits.

"I see. Well, I'm not sure if you'll see many doors closing or yellow-eyed specters, but I'm sure it will be a nice night for all of you." If her story was any indication, it seemed APPS had set the bar quite low in regards to a successful night of ghost hunting.

Lana stood in the doorway and clapped her hands for attention. "Again, welcome to Cider Ridge Inn. I'm Lana and I'll be here to make sure you have everything you need to make your visit memorable." She waved her hand my direction. "You've met my sister, Sunni, the owner of the inn, and as I mentioned to Kenneth, in our phone conversation this morning, she is also a reporter for the *Junction Times*, our local paper. She has been assigned to write an article about APPS. I hope you won't mind her asking questions. We would love for our town to get to know all about the work you do for the paranormal community. And with that, the dinner buffet is ready." As she finished, the lights flickered on and off in the dining room. Everyone sucked in a breath and surveyed the room, apparently looking for ghosts.

"My apologies," I said, "I've had an electrician working—"

Lana coughed into her hand to get my attention. She scowled lightly at me. "What my sister meant to say was you'll find that the Cider Ridge ghost manifests in many different ways. He is quite the prankster." Right then, Edward appeared standing right next to Lana in the doorway. He stared at the side of her face as she finished her explanation of the flickering lights. Seconds later, he disappeared, and I released the breath I'd been holding.

I surveyed the faces around me. No one had noticed any paranormal presence. Thank goodness. It seemed we would get through the night without more than a few tantalizing light flickers and the occasional creaks and moans the house made on its own, without any help from an actual ghost.

CHAPTER 12

*W*hile the group mingled and ate the delicious fare Lana had laid out, I'd gone into my journalistic observation mode. They were so busy discussing and debating paranormal theories, all while piling their plates high with goodies, nobody noticed me jotting down a few notes. Three things stood out as obvious in the group dynamics. Barbara was absolutely and obviously in love with Kenneth Applegate. Which immediately led to my second observation. Kenneth was absolutely and obviously *not* in love with Barbara. In fact, it seemed that his affections were being saved for someone not of this world. He showed both Lana and me the snapshot of the portrait of Lauren Grace, which he kept in his wallet like a man might do with his wife's photo. Even while stuffing his face with Lana's buffet, he spoke on and on about his anticipated stay at Dandelion Inn. The third glaring observation was that Jamie and Kenneth were not on friendly terms. (To put it lightly.)

Jamie wandered around the table a second time with his plate, piling it high again. Kenneth's nostrils flared in disgust. "Are you going to keep eating, Nielson? The rest of us are anxious to explore the house."

That statement caused me to jerk my face Lana's direction. She smiled weakly in response.

"Uh, we'll have to limit it to mostly the downstairs areas," I said hastily. "The stairs are not safe, and a few of the upstairs rooms are a couple thin wood planks away from becoming a downstairs room." I forced a funky little laugh, but my guests didn't share my amusement.

"But, Miss Taylor"—Kenneth looked toward Lana—"mentioned we'd have full access to the house."

"Oh did she?" I tilted my head and skewered my sister with a questioning look.

I could see the industrious gears spinning in my sister's head. "Sunni, how about if you lead up just two people at a time? Surely, the stairs are strong enough for a few people at once. You could stay with them to make sure they avoid dangerous weak spots in the floor." She was on a roll. She moved closer to Kenneth with that salesperson swagger she wore so well. "If you go up in teams, it won't be so intimidating for our resident spirit. He's quite shy and reserved."

My gaze swept the room for my *shy, reserved* ghost, but there was no sign of him. Earlier, he'd hovered around for a few minutes watching the guests eat but then left with a growl, muttering something about the sin of gluttony. I'd found it more than ironic that a group of so-called experts had been sitting under the judgmental gaze of a truly unsettled spirit for a good five minutes but it had not slowed their pursuit of the perfect mashed potato puff or turkey quiche. Although, I did notice Angela Applegate drop a piece of grilled squash when Edward brushed past her at the table. It almost seemed as if she'd felt his presence but, she returned so quickly to her plate, I'd shrugged it off as coincidence. Raine had been right in her harsh review of their skills.

Lana waited, with clasped hands, for everyone to agree with her plan. Growing up with the woman, I knew never to bother disagreeing. During summer breaks, Lana would have our entire days planned and charted before Emily, Neal and I had even rolled out of bed. Eventually, Neal got tired of Lana's activities, like playing pretend school or playing Sea World trainers in the neighbor's pool. (Emily always did an admirable job of playing the part of the seal or otter.) He broke off to do his own thing with his friends. Lana was so hurt she spent a whole week pretending he didn't exist. She went so far as to sit right down on him as he watched television, pretending that he wasn't already in the spot. Emily and I couldn't stop laughing.

Lana's idea was good, only I wished that I hadn't made a fuss at all. The stairs were not that treacherous and the upstairs rooms weren't quite as delicate as I suggested. I just wasn't thrilled about people seeing the overall state of shabbiness. Now, I was stuck leading small group tours rather than just getting the whole thing over with at once. I needed to tweak the plan.

"I'm sure the group would like to tour the upstairs together. If we all stay together and tread carefully, I'm sure we can avoid disaster." I sounded wishy-washy, but it was still better than stretching out the upstairs tours. "You can bring whatever equipment up and get it over with—" I cleared my throat. "I mean you can get the data you need while you're up there, then focus the rest of the evening on the downstairs." I'd gone back on my first objection, but the upstairs really wasn't solid and safe for people to traipse around all night.

Barbara and Angela looked expectantly at Kenneth. From my observations, I'd discovered that both women considered him their leader. Whereas Jamie and Rex were not quite as deferential. Jamie scoffed and rolled eyes at everything Kenneth said. It seemed he wasn't going to wait for the society's namesake to make the decision.

"While all of you decide," Jamie said sharply, "I'm going to get the EVP recorder and head up those stairs. I'm already sensing far more energy coming from above. If we're going to get any data or evidence, it'll be upstairs." He declared it so confidently it was humorous, especially because Edward had materialized in the kitchen again. He drifted in and out of the guests with ease, even stopping to get an up close look at each one of them. I had to hold my breath to keep from laughing.

"I think Sunni is right," Kenneth said, utterly ignoring Jamie's proclamations. "It's best if we stay together, as a group, so we can share experiences as we go. Let's get our equipment." He turned to me. "We'll need the entire house dark for our explorations. We've found that spirits are particularly self-conscious and shy when there is too much light."

Edward found this statement especially amusing. He stepped in front of Kenneth, placed his hand against his stomach and took a deep bow as if waiting for a large applause. I clapped my hands once to show my approval and to get the group's attention.

"The upstairs has no lighting at the moment. I'll have Lana turn off the downstairs lights once we are all safely on the top floor."

Lana was quite disappointed that her individual gift baskets were somewhat of a flop. The ghost hunting team had come prepared with electronic tablets for note taking, night vision goggles and hats with lights that could be easily turned on and off. I, on the other hand, had no such paranormal finery, so I borrowed the flashlight from Angela's basket. I carried along my own journalist notebook and I planned to continue my observations. While the group was busy watching for ghosts, I would be busy watching them.

We lugged ourselves and various devices, including the night vision video camera, digital temperature reader and even a boxy device that used radio frequency to communicate with paranormal entities, up the rickety staircase. We gathered on the landing, and I gave Lana the cue, a short whistle. Seconds later, we were bathed in darkness. I always kept most of the bedroom doors closed, to keep the drafts and unwanted critters from flying into the inhabited rooms in the house. Only one room had leftover furniture, a wrought iron bed frame, a brass light fixture and an old trunk that held a few household and personal items that were embroidered with Bonnie Ross's monogram. There was also a blush inducing, slightly corny love letter written to Bonnie. I was more than certain Edward had written it because the letter had disappeared from my dresser. He'd even broken his golden rule of never entering my 'bedchamber' to take it back.

Small lights went on and devices fired up as the group split off and tiptoed quiet as field mice through the hallways and dark, drafty rooms. As quiet as their practiced footsteps were, Rex did little to keep his thunderous voice from echoing through the emptiness.

"I don't believe that we'll find much up here. Contrary to what Nielsen claimed, I'm not getting any reading at all on the EMF meter."

"Well, we're certainly not going to find any activity with you bellowing through the building and scaring them all off," Nielsen snapped sharply.

"Who is scaring them off now, Nielsen?" Kenneth asked snidely.

I recognized Barbara's soft giggle in the darkness. Even Kenneth's sarcasm was charming to Barbara.

The crew spread out, but Kenneth spotted me standing near the staircase, waiting for them to finish their excursion. He left his team to do the hunting and joined me. "I suppose you don't have much activity since the house was vacant for so long. Now, over at the Dandelion, I understand the beautiful Miss Grace shows herself to guests and staff members regularly. Did I show you the picture I have of her portrait?"

"You did. It's sort of a fun play on words when you say you have a picture of a portrait," I quipped, but he was too busy fishing the picture out of his pocket again. He turned his hat light on and highlighted the photo with its beam.

"They say she was even more lovely in person." He gazed at the picture with such admiration, it was almost touching. (If it hadn't been kind of creepy.) It seemed the man had developed an obsession with the woman's portrait. I almost worried that he might just run into Lauren's ghost and end up forever heartbroken.

Angela and Barbara popped out from the closest bedroom. "Where's Jamie? We need the EMF meter right now," Barbara said, out of breath.

Angela motioned for her brother to come. "It was a strange rush of cold air followed by distinctive footsteps on the wood floors." She was calmer than Barbara, but also had to stop to catch her breath.

Kenneth hopped into action. "Nielsen, get that EMF meter down to this room right away. We've made our first contact." The entire group disappeared into the empty room with their devices and their tablets.

"Bloody fools," Edward drawled next to me.

CHAPTER 13

The Electro Magnetic Field device came up empty in the spare room. The disappointed group of ghost hunters had tromped downstairs with long faces but were immediately cheered when Lana announced she had a special toasted marshmallow milkshake for each one of them.

Raine had decided to stay away, certain that she wouldn't be able to stop herself from asking questions and starting an unfriendly debate. I was relieved. It was one less thing to worry about. It was close to eleven. After the dessert session, I was hoping to slip off to my bedroom. Newman and Redford had taken themselves off hours before when the buffet trays had been covered and put in the refrigerator.

'Lana and her guests sat in the dining room at the tables she had set up for their discussions. Edward had vanished after he witnessed the circus upstairs, and I was just as glad. It seemed we were going to get through the entire night without major incident. The visitors might leave disappointed with the lack of paranormal activity, but I was anxious for the night to run smoothly into a nice, bright fall morning. Then the group would pack up their tools of the trade and move onto the next inn. Maybe Kenneth would have more luck at the Dandelion. If he was really lucky, he'd come face to face with the woman he loved, Lauren Grace.

I carried a stack of plates to the sink to rinse. I hadn't heard the footsteps behind me until I turned off the water.

Angela handed me a few more plates from the table.

"Thanks. How did you like the milkshake?"

"I'm lactose intolerant, but they smelled delicious." She picked up a handful of Lana's party mix and pulled up a chair. I'd asked interview questions intermittently throughout the evening, mostly uninspiring ones like how did you get interested in ghost watching. And most of their answers were as dull and flat as the questions, but I hadn't gotten much chance to talk to Angela alone. She was always busy making sure her brother was the center of attention.

"It must be rather lonely in this big house," Angela said.

I dried my hands and joined her with a fistful of party mix. I pulled out a chair and sat. From what I'd witnessed in my group dynamic observations, Angela was more knowledgeable than her brother about paranormal events. She seemed to be his right hand person, making sure he had everything he needed and ready to assist him at a moment's notice. There wasn't much sibling affection *or* the usual rivalry between them. It was almost as if they'd grown up in separate homes. Angela was a good ten years younger, which might have easily explained why they acted more like business partners than siblings.

"Not too lonely. I have my dogs and both my sisters are just a stroll in either direction." Then, of course, there was another reason why I wasn't the least bit lonely and that reason materialized on the kitchen counter. He looked frazzled from the intrusion into his 'space'. He'd spent so many years wandering the house alone. Since my arrival, it had been nothing but the clamor of construction, dogs barking and playing and constant visitors. I felt a twinge of guilt about causing such a stir in his prison. He couldn't get away from any of it no matter how irritating it all became. It had to be frustrating to know that the quality of his eternity was totally dependent on whoever lived in the house.

"I must say I *do* feel a lot of static charges and changes in temperature in this room in particular." Angela's voice pulled me from my thoughts.

"That might be because it's the kitchen. Plus, I'm having the whole house rewired, so I imagine there are some stray charged particles popping around." I had no real knowledge of electricity, except that it was frustrating when the power was off, but my amateur's explanation sounded plausible to me.

Angela seemed disappointed that I'd dismissed her sixth sense. I back stepped quickly. I was still on the hook for persuading the group to pick Firefly Junction for its convention. "But you're right. I can feel vibrations in the air all the time. Sometimes my dogs just stop and stare at something in the hallway or in another room and when I check it out, there's nothing there."

Her face loosened into a smile. "My dog is very good at sensing invisible entities as well, although sometimes I think he does it just to get my attention. That way I'm reminded that he hasn't had a treat for the last hour. "

"Ah ha, I see our dogs are all from the same family line of treat lovers." I was relieved that my earlier pessimistic comment had been forgotten.

Angela's brow creased. "I have to admit, I thought there would be much more activity in this house than we've experienced. I've read that the spirit left behind died in the vigor of his youth. Then there are those rumors of what his lover told him on his way out of this world. I'm certain that would keep any soul from eternal rest."

I swallowed a large chunk of peanut and put the rest of the

party mix on the table. I looked cautiously around and startled when I found Edward hovering right over my shoulder with a glower that sent a chill through me.

Angela caught my unexplained shiver. "Are you all right, Sunni? You look like you've seen a ghost." She winked at me. "A little paranormal humor."

I forced a dry laugh. "Yes, that's cute." I patted my chest to stop the pain from the peanut going down too fast. "Just need to chew my food better," I said lightly. I took a deep breath, while I debated which way to go. Should I just ignore her comment about the rumors, which more than likely were just more tall tales circulating about the Cider Ridge ghost? Or should I pursue it and find out what she'd heard? If she had something significant, it might help me solve the mystery surrounding Edward's unrest. Of course, pursuing it would have been much less stressful if Edward weren't un-breathing over my shoulder. I would never forgive myself if I let the moment pass without further inquiry.

"You mentioned something about what Edward was told on his death bed?"

"Yes," she said, "Edward was his name. That's what Henrietta told me when I talked to her. She knew quite a lot about the whole tragedy, the duel and the rogue who repaid his cousin's generosity by seducing his young bride."

The air surrounding me grew chilly, but Angela didn't seem to notice the change in temperature.

I had a dozen questions racing through my head. I took another breath to stop myself from overwhelming her with them. I started with the obvious. "Who is Henrietta?"

Angela's eyes rounded. "Henrietta Suffolk? I'm surprised you've never spoken to her. She's a veritable treasure trove of information on this house. I found her when I did my research on haunted houses in the region."

Through Edward's cold aura, I could feel my cheeks warm with shame. I was an investigative journalist, and I had never come across this *veritable treasure trove*. I needed to work on my research skills, it seemed.

"How does Henrietta know so much about Cider Ridge Inn?"

"Henrietta is a sweet woman who lives in Connecticut. She just celebrated her ninety-fifth birthday, but she's as sharp as a tack. She is a direct descendant of Carson Suffolk. Carson was a cousin twice or thrice removed to Cleveland Ross, the man who built this inn."

"Yes, I knew that he built the house," I said, trying to make myself feel better about my apparent ignorance. "How are the Suffolks related to this inn?" I discretely crossed my arms to shield myself from the drop in temperature.

"After the scandalous affair and tragedy that followed, Bonnie was sent to live with the Suffolk family on the east coast. Cleveland wanted nothing to do with her after that."

Edward had drifted farther from the conversation, possibly just to give me a break from the icy air swirling around him. But I had no doubt he was still glued to the conversation at the table. He glided back and forth with a furrowed brow, his image teetering between sharp as a black pen on white paper and as blurry as an unfocused photo.

I contemplated just dropping the subject, but something told me Edward would make a clamor out of frustration.

"Bonnie took care of him after the duel?" I asked.

"Yes, right inside this house. And as the poor man's blood drained away, Henrietta said Bonnie pleaded with him not to leave her. Or at least that was how the story went."

I'd heard the phrase 'how the story went' enough to know to take everything with a grain of salt. A woman pleading with her lover would certainly seem normal during such a dramatic moment. I flicked my gaze Edward's direction. He was deep in thought as he drifted back and forth through the kitchen.

"That all sounds so dramatic and tragic," I added, but I sensed a bigger shoe was about to drop.

"I'm sure it was a very touching scene," she said. "The handsome, roguish man who stole her heart, cut down in his prime by her husband's pistol. And, of course, her heartbreak was only compounded by the pregnancy."

A rush of cool air clattered the pots and pans over the table. Angela's face blanched some and she looked up at the vibrating pots. "What on earth caused that?" she asked.

Edward had shot up to the hearth with a glower that reminded me of a vulture or other angry bird of prey ready to swoop down and cause havoc.

"This is a drafty kitchen," I explained. My stomach tingled with nerves.

Barbara appeared at the kitchen entrance. "There you are, Angela. Kenny wants to have a table discussion about our next adventure at Dandelion Inn. We're hoping to collect quite a bit of data there." It seemed my inn wasn't quite the paranormal hotbed they'd expected. If they only knew.

"I'll be right there," Angela called.

My heart raced ahead, but I couldn't let it end without knowing. "What pregnancy?"

Angela scooted forward like a woman about to relay some juicy gossip. "According to Henrietta, Bonnie was with child, *his* child."

My throat was dry, and it seemed the air in the kitchen was suddenly filled with electrical charges, just like Angela had noted before the conversation turned explosive.

"*His* child?" I asked, but I already knew the answer.

"Yes. Bonnie was pregnant with Edward's baby."

The next few seconds were so fast and alarming, I found it hard to describe them. It was as if an odd explosion, one that came with no flames or blast, burst all the air from the house. The kitchen windows strained, and if the intense pressure had gone on longer, the glass panes would have shattered. Angela and I instinctively covered our ears. There was no loud noise, the opposite, in fact. It felt as if all sound had been vacuumed from the house, and the result left my ears in tight pain as if I was taking off in a plane. Redford and Newman came skittering out of the bedroom with their tails tucked between their legs. They didn't stop until they were both tucked under the table near my feet. When the bizarre shift in air pressure subsided, walls, floors and ceilings relaxed with squeaks as if the air had been released from a balloon. The entire event lasted less than five seconds but a person would have had to be in a coma not to notice it.

"He's here," Angela said breathlessly. "Edward Beckett must be here."

I gathered my wits and glanced back toward the hearth. Only a trail of mist remained where Edward had been hovering.

CHAPTER 14

or a group of self-proclaimed paranormal experts, they were certainly shocked by actual ghostly activity. Angela gasped and stood up so quick, she nearly fell backward over her chair. I caught her arm. Seconds later, alarmed voices and agitated footsteps filled the hallway. Lana was the first person through the kitchen entry. Her flawless skin looked like polished white marble. Her worried gaze shot straight to me. Shocked faces popped up behind her. The entire group, even the confident, arrogant Jamie Nielsen looked pale with fright as they piled into the kitchen.

My hands were shaking as I stuck them behind my back to hide my reaction. "Calm down, everyone. I'm sure there's a good explanation for what just happened."

Barbara was holding tightly to Kenneth's arm. "Like what?" she asked with a trembling voice. "It felt as if someone had squeezed the oxygen out of my lungs." She patted her chest before sidling even closer to Kenneth. It seemed the alarming moment had worked in Barbara's favor.

"A sonic boom," I offered with little confidence.

"I wonder if they're doing any logging up in the mountains right now," Lana suggested.

I pointed at her. "Yes, Lana's right," I said too loudly. I steadied my voice. "I'm sure there is some logging happening nearby, and it shook the house."

Rex Thunder wasn't buying our flimsy explanations. "Lumberjacks have a dangerous enough job in full daylight. I can't imagine any of them would be foolhardy enough to cut timber in the dead of night. Besides, it was more a change in air pressure than a booming sound. It felt as if the entire house had been submerged deep in the ocean and then brought to the surface too quickly. Like divers experience on their way to the top."

Lana gave me a wry half smile, apparently hoping I'd come up with something else. But I had nothing.

Jamie had finally gathered his wits. "I'm going to turn on the EMF meter and the electronic voice recorder. It certainly seems as if we've just experienced a significant paranormal event."

Lana scooted closer to me and whispered from the side of her mouth. "What on earth is going on? Even the dogs look freaked out."

Their fur had smoothed and their tails were no longer anchored between their legs, but Redford and Newman seemed committed to spending the rest of the night under the kitchen table.

"Can't explain it." I hated lying. I especially hated lying to my sister. Unfortunately, ever since Edward introduced himself to me, I'd had to stretch, bend, fudge and laugh off the truth. It was stressful, but tonight took that stress to a whole new level.

Kenneth managed to pry his arm free from Barbara's death grip. He and Rex decided to take a quick tour of the downstairs.

Barbara, who never let Kenneth out of her sight, followed

closely at their heels. Angela decided to join Jamie on his survey with the magnetic field reader.

Lana hurried to the refrigerator. "Fortunately, I have a midnight snack of peanut butter cookies and hot cocoa planned. That should take their minds off the unsettling—" She pulled the milk out of the refrigerator. "I don't even know what to call it. For a second there, I thought the entire house was going to be sucked up into an alien spaceship. I swear it felt as if my skin was being pulled back to my ears like a facelift. And the hairs on my arms stood straight up."

She pulled my crock pot out from the pantry shelf and got straight to work on the midnight snack. It took a lot to throw Lana off her game. She even managed to do a respectable job catering a bridal party turned murder investigation in the middle of the national park.

"Sunni, you can go to bed. I know you have to get up early for work."

"Technically, I'm at work." I glanced back to make sure no one was in ear shot, then moved closer to Lana. She began grating a large block of dark chocolate. "I'm supposed to be writing a glowing narrative about the ghost hunting team, but it's hard to work up too many flattering phrases about a group of people who were scared witless at the first sign of a disturbance."

Lana lowered the block of chocolate and looked at me. "Do you think it was some kind of—you know—ghostly disturbance?"

"What? No. What? I mean, what do I know?" I grabbed a pinch of chocolate and pushed it between my lips to shut me up.

"It was the strangest thing I've ever experienced but it didn't last long. Maybe you were right about a sonic boom. Maybe some Air Force jets were flying overhead," Lana suggested.

I licked a crumb of chocolate off my bottom lip. "I'm sure that's all it was."

She went back to her grating. "Still, we could certainly let them go on thinking that your Cider Ridge ghost was giving them some kind of signal. I mean, it can't hurt. They came here for that reason. Might even help them decide to come back here for the convention."

I lowered my chin and peered up at her. "Lana, I love you and I wish you great success, but I'm not hosting an entire convention of ghost hunters in this house."

"No, of course not. It's not nearly finished enough for that."

Angela walked back into the kitchen. The color had returned to her cheeks. She walked straight to me with a question. "Do you think I caused that stir by mentioning that Bonnie Ross was pregnant?" She was proving more and more to be the most astute and dialed in person of the group, although something told me her older brother never noticed that.

"The scandal produced an illegitimate baby?" Lana piped up from behind her pile of grated chocolate. "That certainly adds another layer to the mystery."

The last thing I wanted was for the topic of Bonnie's pregnancy to take flight again. There was no telling what Edward would do if we dwelled on the subject. As it was, I had no idea where he'd sulked off to, and I had a house full of strangers who badly wanted to lure him out from his hiding spot.

I turned to Angela. "We aren't even certain the incident had anything to do with a ghost. But I thank you for filling me in on some of the gritty history of this place. It's always interesting to hear details. Lana is making a crock pot of hot cocoa to go with her special peanut butter cookies. I know you mentioned you're lactose intolerant."

Lana sighed loudly. "That's right. I completely forgot. Can I make you some hibiscus tea to go with the cookies or maybe a glass of wine?"

Angela nodded. "A glass of wine would be nice." She held up her hand. It trembled slightly. "I'm still recuperating from the entire incident. I was certain I'd angered or upset Edward with my revelation."

"Nonsense. I've been meaning to do some more digging into the inn's past, but, if I'm being totally honest, I haven't had time or the patience," I said. "I'd love to get the contact information for Henrietta Suffolk so I can ask her a few questions."

"Yes, of course," Angela said.

I hurried to the refrigerator for the bottle of wine Lana had stored inside. It had been a trying night and a glass of pinot noir would help me sleep, but I needed to stay awake and alert. Once my guests had settled down for the night, and I feared that wouldn't be for hours, I needed to go in search of Edward. As rough as my night had been, it was nothing compared to his. His overwhelming reaction to the news of Bonnie's pregnancy assured me he'd known nothing about it.

CHAPTER 15

*A*pparently, even hardened ghost hunters had their limits when it came to staying up past midnight. Once Lana made sure everyone had full bellies and everything they needed for a comfy night, she went home to bed.

The team had scoured the downstairs, and after a great deal of pleading with the owner of the inn, the upstairs, to discover the source for the strange anomaly during the marshmallow milkshake break. They came up empty handed and eventually took their deflated frowns and trudging, tired feet to bed.

I was far too worried to sleep. I sat in my bed reading the same line of my book a dozen times as I listened for a dozy silence to seep through the house. After the scare, Redford and Newman had both decided to crawl not only on top of the bed but under my blankets. I carefully removed my legs, not wanting to disturb them. It was impossible to sneak quietly around a house full of guests with eight sets of claws click-clacking on the hard floor.

I'd worn my sweatpants and a t-shirt to bed in case one of the guests needed something or in case of trouble. My slippers tended to make slapping sounds as I walked around the house, so I ventured out of the room in bare feet.

I tiptoed to the kitchen. (Not that tiptoeing made much sense in a house with interminably squeaky floors.) It was colder than I expected, even wearing my *glamorous* sweatpants. I stood by the hearth, Edward's favorite perch, and rubbed warmth into my arms while I waited. After a few impatient minutes, I loudly whispered his name. "Edward, do you want to talk?"

There was no response or sign of him. I crept quietly through the hallway and peeked in on the guests. Everyone had burrowed under the lush bed quilts and pillows. The only sound came from Rex Thunder who was brewing up some real thunder with his snores.

I peeked into the sitting room just past the dining room. It was the one room that had been entirely restored. Occasionally I poked my head inside for encouragement to remind myself how beautiful the place would look when it was finished. My first tussle with Edward came when I'd set my mind on painting the room cupid pink. He disagreed vehemently. We eventually settled on an elegant dove gray. I figured, if nothing else, it was nice to be haunted by a ghost with good fashion sense and stylish taste.

There was no sign of Edward. I couldn't even feel his presence, something that usually happened when he was about to materialize in the same room. As I walked lightly back to the kitchen, I heard a noise above me. It was just light enough to almost miss and just loud enough to let me know something was happening upstairs. I turned back and tried to walk with feather light footsteps up the rickety steps.

I'd developed more than a sixth sense when it came to Edward. I could feel changes in the air temperature and even silent vibrations whenever he was upset about something. In the darkness blanketing the upper level of the house, that extra sense led me to the room where the remnants of Cleveland Ross's furnishings remained. A broken bed frame, a fallen light fixture and an old trunk made up the leftovers of the bleak Ross history. And even bleaker was my incorporeal friend.

Edward was perched on the window sill staring out into the shadowy night. Enough moonlight streaked through the dusty window to let me see the grim expression in his wavering image. He heard me walk in but kept his focus on the yard. He was a striking figure in his fawn colored breeches, black Hessian boots and waistcoat. Even in a vaporous state, he had a strong, masculine profile. Certainly, Bonnie Ross suffered a great deal of heartbreak once Edward Beckett strolled into her life. And tonight, we learned just how much sorrow she'd endured.

I wiped the dust off the trunk and sat down. "I'm guessing you didn't know that Bonnie was pregnant with your child."

His image tended to fade in and out when he was upset, but it was clear and sharp at the moment. "I *did* know. I'd just pushed it out of my mind. Until tonight." He drew his gaze away from the window and looked at me. "When are those witless bunch of trespassers leaving?" In general, Edward didn't care for visitors, but he was particularly irritated with the Applegate Society.

He turned back to the window. "I feel like an animal exhibit in the zoo, and they are the silly people looking through the bars waiting for the bear or lion to do his trick."

"Well, they certainly got more show than they expected. Or than I expected." I tried a cheerier tone, but that didn't seem to help.

"Yes, and weren't they a courageous lot of ghost seekers," he snapped. "Half expected them to gather up their ridiculous machines and scurry out into the night."

I chuckled. "They did fall apart some when confronted with an actual paranormal event, didn't they?"

His expression loosened. "Thought that one man with the odd open shoes was going to throw up from fear."

"Yes, Jamie Nielsen did look slightly green around the gills when he raced into the kitchen. But he did bravely search the house with his electromagnetic field meter. Oddly enough, the machine didn't detect anything."

"Electromagnetic," he repeated quite artfully. "What an outlandish century you live in where people just string together long syllables and important sounding words to pretend expertise."

"I don't remember much from my high school physics, but I don't think it's as complex as it sounds. Have you been up here since that pivotal moment in the kitchen?"

"Pivotal? I don't know this word but if you're referring to the moment when the woman with the severe black hair blurted to the world that I'd fathered a—" He stopped short of saying the brutal word, a word that was used to shame people back in his day. Thankfully, that had fallen out of vogue through the centuries. "Yes, I've been up here in this dingy box of a room, the room where I perished."

I stared up at him, my mouth agape. It had somehow never occurred to me to ask which room he'd been carried to on that fateful day. It was selfish and more than a tad thoughtless of me never to bring it up. "You died here in this room?"

His nod was slow and faint. "Stared at that blasted brass light fixture for hours waiting for the pain and misery to end."

I looked over at the brass ceiling lamp. It had eight tarnished arms reaching out from a bulbous center like a brass covered octopus. The glass shades that protected the candles were long gone, splintered into dust over the years. The fixture still wore a crown of ceiling plaster. "You pulled it down from the ceiling," I said.

"Yes, as I watched them carry my body out of the room, it occurred to me that I was still stuck in the house. Or what was left of me. I got angry and used my new invisible strength to pull it down. Scared everyone near to death," he said with a weak smile. "But they weren't nearly as scared as I was."

His words felt heavy on my chest. I had never seen him so sullen, and it worried me plenty. It was up to me to help him find his way. I wasn't a hundred percent positive, but it seemed as if we'd turned a corner in the mystery of his eternal imprisonment in Cider Ridge Inn.

"Edward, I'm carrying your child," he muttered toward the window panes again. As arrogant and outspoken and at ease as he was when talking to me, it seemed it was hard for him to face me on this subject. "What woman tells a dying man those words as he's leaving his earthly form?"

"Those were her last words?" I asked. "Bonnie told you that as you took your last breath?"

"I can remember it clearly now. I'd wiped them away, hoping that I'd only imagined them. But it's true. She confessed seconds before my lids fell shut."

I stood up and walked to the window. The moon and nightly breeze were playing tricks on the shadows, making trees look like long armed monsters and the grass look like the rippling waves of a stormy ocean. "I know this is upsetting, Edward, but I think this has opened the door to us finding out why you never moved on."

He turned to me.

I continued. "You said you weren't sure why you were stuck inside the inn. I think this might be it. You left this world never knowing what happened to your child. That's a pretty heavy thing to take with you. It's definitely something that might be holding you back. Don't you think?"

My revelation made his image waver, fade and then return sharply. "You're right, Sunni. I'd swept the whole thing away and forgotten all about those last few, devastating words. But how will this help me? How can I possibly ever find out what happened to Bonnie's baby? It's been over two hundred years."

I smiled. "And that's exactly how we can find out. We are in a new century. And we'll start with that strange metal box that you like to complain I stare at far too often. And I've also got the name of an elderly woman who was related to the cousin who took Bonnie in when Cleveland sent her away. She seems to know a lot about the entire story. I'll contact her just as soon as I have time. Before you know it, we'll have you off enjoying a nice, relaxing eternity."

His laugh had a dark edge to it. "You and I have different opinions about which eternity is waiting for me. Mine doesn't include nice or relaxing."

I rubbed my chin for a second. "Hmm, never thought of that. Well, let's see where the research takes us and worry about that later."

CHAPTER 16

*A*fter a long night, the aroma of bacon frying was like a shot of adrenaline. I sat up, still groggy, and rubbed my face to wake myself up. Newman and Redford were at the bedroom door, whining and wagging tails, anxious to follow the delicious smell to its source.

I stood from my bed and stared down at my sweatpants. The entire night came back to me in one dizzying swoop. I sat down hard on the mattress. Redford trotted over and scratched me sharply on the shin.

"Ouch, yes, I know, bacon, bacon, bacon. Whatever you do, don't worry about your favorite dog mom looking peaked and lightheaded." I walked to the door and opened it. The dogs raced out. I returned to the bed and sat down. The rich smells coming from the kitchen assured me that Lana was already taking care of the guests. I'd wisely mentioned to Parker that I'd be in late because the Applegate Society was staying the night.

I flopped back on the mattress and stared at the ceiling. I had my work cut out for me, and not just in writing a glowing article about a group of paranormal experts who nearly fainted during a brief encounter with a ghost. The kicker was that they didn't even realize it was Edward. No proof showed up on any of their equipment. The entire strange event could have been easily explained away by a sonic boom or rapid change in barometric pressure. Those were two of the theories being bandied about when their equipment found no evidence of paranormal activity. On top of making sure to write a compelling article, I had now taken it upon myself to find out what happened to Bonnie Ross and her baby. I was glad to have a place to start, but it seemed that a quick and easy 'ah ha' moment to explain Edward's situation was not going to be quick or easy.

A light knock on the door was followed by Lana's smiling face. Her skin glowed and her eyes sparkled as if she'd slept through a long, glorious night. Which she no doubt had after she left the inn. "I'm making omelets and I forgot my shallots. Do you have any?"

I sat up. "You're at the wrong sister's house. You might as well ask if I have any truffles. I wouldn't know what to do with a shallot if I had one." I lowered my feet to the floor.

Lana walked inside the room and put her hands on her hips. "Why do you look like you just returned from an all night rock concert? Nice sleepwear, by the way."

"Not in the mood for big sister sarcasm this morning. It was a long night." I tromped over to my dresser.

"Oh, why was it so long? It seemed everyone was getting settled in after the odd air pressure thing. Did you ever find the source of it?"

"No. It's an old house. Every day is an adventure of oddities. I just meant it was long because I'm not used to having strangers in the house. I didn't sleep well."

Lana came over and hugged me. "I know and I appreciate the sacrifice. Now get dressed and come out to breakfast so you can see your guests off. They are packing up to head to Dandelion Inn right after a shopping excursion in town."

I pulled a pair of pants and a sweater out of the dresser. "I sure don't have much for an article yet. I might have to visit them at Dandelion Inn. Maybe there'll be more suitable ghost activity there so I can *watch* the experts in action."

"Thought you weren't in the mood for sarcasm," Lana quipped before walking out.

I quickly showered and changed. If nothing else, I needed to get to the kitchen to make sure a certain ghost wasn't skulking acting broody and mad. He didn't seem terribly convinced that I'd be able to find out what happened to his baby. It was possible he didn't even want to know. Pregnancy and giving birth were dangerous back then. I'd hate to discover that Bonnie died in childbirth. Then Edward would be saddled with the knowledge that his sordid affair with Bonnie resulted in her death. That thought sent nervous flutters through my stomach as I headed toward the voices in the kitchen.

Angela looked up from her cup of coffee. Barbara, Kenneth and Rex had joined her at the kitchen table. Naturally, Barbara was glued to Kenneth's side, gazing starry eyed at him as he drank his coffee.

There was no sign of Edward. My shoulders sank a good two inches with relief. As usual, Lana had pulled out all the stops. Fresh blueberry muffins sat on a platter in the center of the pine table. Her freshly churned butter was mounded into a silver chafing dish.

"By the way, Sunni—" Lana pointed to a large envelope on the corner of the counter stamped 'do not bend'. "The mailman couldn't fit that in the mailbox."

The return address was from Lola's Antiques in Port Danby. My pictures had arrived. I left them on the counter. As much as I wanted to look at them, I decided to wait for my visitors to leave. I was just about to reach for a cup of coffee when I heard Raine's familiar giggle through the kitchen window. I leaned over the sink and peered out. If I tilted my head just enough, I could see the right half of the front porch. Raine was leaning against the railing talking animatedly to Jamie. He was wearing a red and blue flannel shirt over a black turtle neck.

I returned to my pursuit of hot coffee. I needed to ingratiate myself this morning to make sure I could join APPS on their next adventure, or my article would be a few, skeletal paragraphs.

I sat down with the coffee and grabbed a blueberry muffin. "I hope everyone slept comfortably. I know the house moans and groans a lot."

Rex followed my lead and took a muffin. "Old bones make you do that," he chuckled. "I can't stand up from a couch without a chorus of groans."

Kenneth patted his flecked beard with his napkin before dropping it on his lap. "I've told you, Rex, you need to eat better. You're still eating burgers, fries and spicy food like you're twenty. A good healthy diet will take those aches right out of your bones."

Angela's pale skin looked extra translucent in the light coming through the window. She had pulled her black hair back into a ponytail. She seemed amused by her brother's condescending lecture. "Thank you for asking, Sunni," Angela said. "The accommodations were wonderful. Once we calmed our nerves after the unusual incident, I think we all slept well."

"Might have been easier if Rex hadn't snored like a buffalo," Jamie said as he walked into the kitchen. Raine was right behind him with a flirty smile still plastered on her face.

"Raine, could you help me carry the plates to the table," Lana called from the stove.

"Sure."

"None for me, Raine," I said. "The muffin is plenty."

After omelets were delivered, Raine sat across from Jamie and next to me. She wasted no time. "Jamie tells me there was a strange change in air pressure, like a quiet implosion, in the house last night." She buttered a muffin.

"Yes," I said.

"Is that all you can say about it?" Raine asked.

I wiped butter from my mouth and sipped coffee. "Yep. Pretty much. Not sure how to elaborate. Jamie's description is accurate."

"Was it Edward?" Raine asked.

"You know I don't much about that kind of stuff, Raine." I was desperate to move on to a new topic. I turned to Kenneth. "I hope you don't mind if I drop by Dandelion Inn today for a few interviews. As I mentioned, I'm the person assigned to writing an article on your society for the *Junction Times*. I've already met the owner of Dandelion—"

Kenneth nearly choked on his tongue. "You've seen her? You've communicated with Lauren Grace?"

Angela grinned meekly as she touched her brother's arm. "I think she means the current owner, Kitty Bloomfield."

Jamie hid a smile behind his napkin. Fortunately, since everyone was fidgeting from the awkward moment, he didn't take the opportunity to mock or tease Kenneth about his strange assumption. He certainly had the ghost of Lauren Grace caught firmly in his head and heart. What a ridiculous notion to have a crush on a ghost. Then I immediately wondered what Edward was up to.

Kenneth's face tinted red from embarrassment, which morphed into a grouchy response. "I certainly hope you'll mention to your readers the brief but alarming event that took place last night and how professional and skilled we were at handling it."

I was taken aback by the tone of his question. It was almost threatening. He knew, too well, that his entire team of paranormal experts had been frightened by Edward's stunt. It would have been difficult to label their response professional or skilled. Lana favored me with an imploring pair of puppy dog eyes. She'd worked so hard to make their visit wonderful, I didn't want to let her down.

"Why, of course. I'll mention how courageously and quickly you pulled out your equipment to gather data," I added.

Jamie puffed a sound from his mouth. "Lot of good that did us. Not one move of the dial. Not one blip on the screen. I'm not convinced it was a paranormal event at all. Maybe she shouldn't even mention it. I'd hate for Evanmore's Ghostly Heritage Society to find out we overreacted to a sonic boom, or worse, the settling bones of an old house."

"Nonsense. Of course it was something from the spirit world," Kenneth said confidently. "And you may visit us at Dandelion Inn. We'll try and make time for some interviews. As long as you don't get in the way of our research. The lovely—" He cleared his throat. "The lingering spirit in Dandelion Inn has a very strong presence, and we expect to be quite busy gathering data." It seemed the last comment was somewhat of a ding against my seemingly un-haunted inn.

After breakfast, Lola and Raine helped the visitors get ready to leave. I had a few minutes alone in the kitchen while luggage and gear was being carried out of the house. Curiosity got the best of me. I picked up the envelope of pictures from Lola's Antiques. I slid them out. The first picture was a bucolic scene of kids playing croquet on the front lawn with their mother watching on from the porch. I slid my eyes over to the smear and focused. I had not imagined it. It was Edward, staring back at me from the porch. The photographer had probably passed off the smudged image as a mistake in processing.

"Is that—" Jamie Nielsen's deep voice dribbled over my shoulder.

My heart raced as I jammed the picture back into the envelope. "Yes, it's a picture of the inn mid nineteenth century."

"But it looked—" Again, I didn't let him finish.

"If you'll excuse me, I've got to get ready for work." I raced down the short hallway to my bedroom and put the pictures on the dresser. I stayed in my room until I heard their car drive away. My pulse slowed as I easily convinced myself Jamie hadn't seen enough to give it another thought.

CHAPTER 17

*K*itty Bloomfield was, once again, overly gracious. Not only did she welcome me in to interview her guests, she'd set aside a quiet sitting room for it. I was spending far more time making mental notes of the wonderful Dandelion Inn than I was thinking about my interview questions. Lana had spent so much time treating the group to her various party yummies, my notes from the previous night were mostly observational. I needed some noteworthy quotes, and those could only be gained through a formal interview. Fortunately, the lush decor of feathery embossed wallpaper, supple wingback chairs and the constant scent of cinnamon and citrus from a bowl of potpourri made the formal interview feel much more informal. Although my first interviewee, Jamie Nielsen, sat ramrod straight in the chair as if he didn't appreciate being questioned about his purported *talents*. Up to this point, his answers had been curt, succinct and, for the most part, uninspiring. He preferred the scientific side to the metaphysical aspects of ghost hunting.

Jamie rubbed the auburn goatee on his strong chin as he waited for my next question.

"When did you first gain an interest in paranormal preservation? And exactly what does the preservation term in the society mean?"

"Surely you've heard Applegate's inane motto of helping spirits lead full un-lifes. Frankly, I'm in this society only until I can get the following and time to start my own. It will be a highly science and data driven group."

"Do you think that ghost hunting is a matter of having the right equipment and being in the right place at the right time?"

"Yes, well, not entirely." He had his long hair wrapped into a bun at the back of his head, making it awkward for him to rest his head back against the tall chair. He straightened his posture again. "It takes a good deal of extra sensory perception to be able to locate the spirits. After that, scientific data can be used to prove their existence. Especially for people like yourself who don't possess the sixth sense."

I stifled a smile. If only I could just spill it all. Wouldn't that send his little man bun into a spinning top. "I see. So in order to be successful in ghost hunting, you must have extra sensory perception."

"Yes, I believe so. There are plenty who pretend to have it, but they are generally just good actors."

"Good actors?"

"Yes, they shriek and gasp and claim to feel cold rushes of air or icy fingers on their arm, but I can tell you there are three times as many fakes as there are true experts."

With his permission, I was taping the conversation, but I tended to do a lot of note jotting as well. Especially when it was something of interest. Nielsen's interview was probably too controversial to add to what was supposed to be a glowing story on the society, but I would manage to politely fit in a few of his comments.

Barbara opened the door and walked into the room. She startled and her cheeks turned pink. "Oh, I'm sorry. I thought it was my turn."

"We are almost done here, Barbara," I said. "I'll come fetch you when we're through."

"Great. I'll just be having tea in the dining room." She hurried back out.

Jamie looked even more bored than when we started. I decided to make it the last question. Since he was so certain he had the extra sense, the one that allowed him to experience and see things us *regular* five sense people couldn't, I thought I'd ask him about the incident at Cider Ridge.

"One last question, if you don't mind. What do you think happened last night at Cider Ridge Inn? What's your general *sense* of the incident? Do you feel somewhere in that extra honed perception of yours that it was caused by an unsettled spirit or something that had nothing to do with the supernatural?"

"My senses and expert background on all things supernatural assure me it was some weather shift or your house settling or even possibly your own suggestion of a jet flying faster than sound and causing shock waves. But it wasn't a ghost. If it had been my equipment would have picked it up. Like I said, true paranormal research requires a sixth sense and a heaping dose of science."

I was becoming expert at using my poker face with Mr. Nielsen. I finished a few notes. "Thank you so much and I hope I didn't waste too much of your time."

His face took on a wholly more interested expression as he sat forward. "Since I answered your questions," he said. "May I ask you one as well?"

I wasn't sure which way this was going. "Sure," I said tentatively.

"About those pictures I saw you holding—"

I pushed out a frilly laugh. "Just some old photoshopped pictures of the inn a friend sent. They're nothing."

He nodded half-heartedly and got up from the chair. I waited for him and caught my breath at the same time. I had no idea if he bought my photoshop explanation. I was just glad to be done with the interview. I double checked that my recorder was working, then I set out to find Barbara. She'd mentioned tea. I crossed paths with the young, energetic housekeeper, Wilma Knowles, on my way to the dining room. She was carrying a vacuum through to the next room.

"Hello, are you enjoying your stay here at the Dandelion?" she asked. "Any sign of Lauren Grace yet?"

"Actually, I'm with the *Junction Times*. I'm writing an article about the group."

"Oh, right, I saw you yesterday having tea with Kitty. Welcome again." She tromped off with her vacuum. The daily cleaning ritual wasn't something I'd wrapped my mind around yet. There was so much to think about before opening an inn.

I walked through to the dining room. Barbara sipped her cup of tea, but her focus was on something across the room. Naturally, it was Kenneth. And even more predictably, Kenneth was standing in front of the hearth gazing adoringly up at the portrait of Lauren Grace.

"Barbara, I'm ready if you're finished with your tea," I said.

She dragged her gaze away from Kenneth. "Of course." She tipped the tea cup back to finish it and clinked the cup down on the saucer. "Kenny, I'll just be in the next room being interviewed if you need me." She patted her mouth with her napkin and got up from the chair.

Kenneth looked over at us as if he'd just noticed the two of us standing in the same room. "Isn't she something?" He pointed up at the portrait as he addressed me.

"She is very lovely. I hope you'll catch a good glimpse of her during your stay." Just as we were about to exit, Angela walked into the dining room.

"Hello, Sunni," she said before turning to her brother. "I thought I might find you here, Ken. I can't find the notes you gave me to put up on the blog. I've looked all over for them."

Kenneth grunted in frustration. "I put them right on the dresser," he barked.

"I've checked my dresser," Angela insisted.

"No, I meant the dresser in my bedroom." He shook his head as if the miscommunication was Angela's fault when it clearly rested with him.

Angela smiled weakly at us as she hurried back out of the room.

"He's very tense about this visit," Barbara whispered as she followed behind me. "He's been waiting to meet Lauren Grace for some time. And I'm sure we will see her soon. We can all sense her presence." We walked along the corridor to the sitting room. "It's quite obvious that there is a lot of paranormal activity in this house."

We reached the sitting room. I motioned for her to sit across from me on the leather chair.

"So there is much more activity here than at Cider Ridge?" I asked. Sometimes I was a touch wicked, but there had to be some bonus to living with a secret ghost.

Barbara was a small, fidgety woman and the tall, wingback chair nearly swallowed her as she scooted back to get comfortable. Her feet no longer touched the ground and they swung lightly back and forth. "Oh, yes, I'm afraid we were somewhat disappointed at the lack of it in your inn." She covered her mouth for a second then lowered her fingers. "I hope you don't find that insulting. It's a lovely home. Well, it will be once you've finished it. But

I'm afraid it's just not haunted, or at least not highly active like the haunted house register claims."

I pointed out my recorder. "Do you mind if I record our chat? That way I can spend more time listening and less time writing."

"Of course. I don't mind at all."

"I guess this register I've heard mentioned is a list of houses in America that are known to be haunted by restless spirits."

"Yes, it's a very long list and your house, Cider Ridge Inn, falls in the highly active section of the list. Kenneth mentioned that he might ask the board that updates the list to move your inn to mildly active. I hope that won't be a problem for you. If it is, then I'll speak to him." Her cheeks rounded. "Kenny and I are very close."

"Yes, I've noticed you spend a great deal of time together." Unfortunately, it seemed like a one-way friendship but then maybe I didn't know the whole story. "Barbara, when did you first get interested in ghost hunting?"

"I prefer to call it ghost watching, you know like bird watching. Hunting has such a harsh connotation."

"True. Good point."

"To be honest, I'd never thought twice about spirits or paranormal activity until I happened upon Kenny's YouTube program. He was so confident and well-spoken." She was practically gushing with admiration as she spoke. "And such an expert. I was a true believer after just two episodes."

I nodded. "Yes, I was doing some research for the article. I caught a few minutes of his show. He's very knowledgeable." I'd come across Kenneth Applegate's series but couldn't force myself to watch more than a few minutes. I found it uninspiring and dull. It seemed Barbara'd had the opposite reaction. "Do you think you have the sixth sense that Jamie Nielsen talks about, or did you just join because you found Ken's videos interesting?"

"I do think I have some of that sixth sense." She spoke of it as if she was talking about having some sugar in her kitchen cabinet. "It comes and goes, but as I've told Kenny, it gets much stronger when he is near." She blushed pink.

"I suppose that's why you stay so close to him. You are refining that extra sensory perception," I said.

"Yes, of course. I want to be an exceptional ghost watcher just like Kenny."

CHAPTER 18

My day had been even more uninspiring than Kenneth Applegate's online series. I'd come to the conclusion that the Applegate Paranormal Preservation Society was little more than a mingling of people with varied knowledge and talent in the area of ghosts. They had few significant experiences to share, but all the while, each person was convinced that they were an authority on the subject. Angela Applegate seemed to have the most knowledge, but she, too, had experienced few notable encounters with the spirit world.

I was relieved when Raine invited herself to dinner at my house. I needed some relaxation and fun. At her request, we'd rolled out a store-bought pizza dough and topped it with an obscene amount of cheese and pepperoni.

I pulled the slice of pizza from my mouth, and for the hundredth time, found myself still attached to the slice by a string of mozzarella. I kept slurping it in, but finally had to reach up and break the tenacious cheese with my fingers to get free of my pizza.

I swallowed the bite. "We might have gone just a tad too far with the cheese."

Raine was struggling with her own cheese tether as she shook her head in disagreement. "No such thing as too much cheese. That's like saying the pancakes have too much maple syrup or the corn has too much butter. Can't be done." She sat back with the grin of a cat that'd just finished an entire plate of trout. "I'm full though. Couldn't eat another bite."

"That's a shame because I bought mint chip ice cream for dessert," I said.

"My dinner stomach is full. There's plenty of room in my dessert stomach."

I laughed hard enough to nearly slip off the kitchen stool. "Boy, I needed this. It's been a long, tiring night and day. And I'm going back to Dandelion Inn at ten tonight. They are doing a special summoning session to see if they can get Lauren Grace to materialize."

Raine rolled her eyes. "Oh please. It'll never work. They don't have what it takes. They are all about contraptions and measuring vibrations and temperature changes. According to them, every draft is a ghost reaching out to them for help."

"But I thought you were convinced that Jamie Nielsen was the real deal. He certainly thinks that. Or was it just that he's tall and nice looking and he wears Birkenstock sandals?"

Raine pushed her glasses higher on her nose. "Not going to lie. I came to that same shallow conclusion after Jamie and I talked this morning. Up until then, I'd only heard him speak at book signings. But listening to him drone on about EMFs and these new boxes that allow them to capture ghost conversations through vibrations, I realized I was more interested in his cool goatee than his knowledge. So, there you have it. Your best friend shuns substance for broad shoulders and a nice beard."

For the first time since our talk in the upstairs bedroom the night before, Edward made his appearance. He drifted up to his perch on the hearth. His face was much less contorted with worry. I hoped that the shock about his fathering Bonnie's baby had worn off.

"Speaking of broad shoulders—" Raine hopped up to get the ice cream from the refrigerator. "Have you seen the town's dashing detective since Monday's lunch?"

That question caught Edward's full attention. Detective Jackson had shown up to the house a few times, and Edward had taken an instant dislike to the man. A strange thing had happened on one of Jackson's visits. Edward had blurted out one of his sarcastic remarks, meant only for my ears, but it seemed Jackson had heard him. It made no sense at the time, especially because Ursula and Henry were in the same room and they hadn't heard a word.

I raised my chin at Edward before answering Raine. "As a matter of fact, I ran into him yesterday morning at the coffee shop."

Raine carried the ice cream and two bowls back with her. "And how did that go?"

"You'd have to ask the pretty redhead he was with to find out for sure."

Raine's posture deflated. She'd set her mind on Jackson and me becoming an item, but I was pretty sure she'd be waiting a long time to see that. She pried open the ice cream carton. "That's too bad. Although that's sort of his thing."

"Redheads?" I asked.

"No. A multitude of pretty women."

"Oh." I didn't bother looking toward Edward since he'd already expressed his distaste for my detective friend. Although, the irony of how many character traits they shared was not lost on me. "I didn't talk to Lana today. Did she feel confident about how things went here?"

"I'm not sure. She thought they enjoyed themselves. Even if the resident ghost didn't make his appearance. But, I'm not convinced he didn't. She told me all about that weird change in air pressure. Sounds like he was mad about something. Maybe he didn't like having so many strangers in his house."

Edward floated closer, apparently entertained by her theories. Raine paused as he neared. It almost seemed as if she sensed something but then she continued. "I'm not surprised he didn't make himself known. I've already deduced that he is either too shy or too arrogant to bother with any of us."

Edward tilted his head side to side showing he approved of this conclusion. I found it amusing how Raine had so easily understood his arrogance without ever meeting him.

I finished my last bite of ice cream. "I suppose I should get ready to head back to Dandelion Inn. Maybe Kitty Bloomfield's ghost is less arrogant than mine and she'll make an appearance. That'll help secure their decision to hold the convention here in town."

Raine stood up with me and helped me carry dishes to the sink. "I wouldn't count on those silly people to conjure up anything except dust bunnies and a lot of paranormal hooey." She stopped. "Hooey? When did I turn into my mom? Anyhow, don't expect much tonight."

"You never know. Something exciting might happen. Then I'll actually have something interesting to write for the paper."

CHAPTER 19

*I*t certainly didn't take a sixth sense or clairvoyant skills to know something was amiss at Dandelion Inn. Flashing red lights splashed glowing shadows over the property, causing the Victorian style house to look more sinister than delightful. An ambulance waited, its rear door wide open, at the top of the driveway. The remainder of the curbside was taken up by a fire truck, a paramedic truck and two police cars.

I pulled past the chaotic scene and parked my jeep in front of the next house. Curious and stunned neighbors had wandered out from their houses, some in pajamas and robes, to see what was happening. I walked past one woman who had pulled a snow parka over a pair of pink pajamas. She was holding her cat. The animal didn't seem the least bit frightened of all the activity.

"Do you know what's happened?" I asked her.

"No idea." She stroked her cat's head. "I'll bet that terrible ghost has been up to no good. I hear she likes to play tricks on the guests. Maybe someone had a heart attack from fright," she suggested. It was plain to see that she was making up a scenario as she went.

I forged ahead. As a reporter, I'd learned that if you appear confident, emergency personnel tend to assume you belong at the scene. I strode up the driveway past several firemen talking on the front lawn. They looked my direction.

"Evening," I said calmly and kept walking right up the front steps and through the open front door. I was immediately met with a distressing sight. Rex and Jamie were doing their best to console Angela, who was bent over with sobs.

"How can it be?" she groaned between sniffles. Her face was red and wet from crying. "We were just finishing up with his latest blog post. It's not possible."

Jamie spotted me in the foyer. "Miss Taylor? When did you arrive?"

Angela peered up from her hunched over position just long enough to see me. She immediately covered her face and crumpled into sobs again.

Jamie left his position at her right side, allowing Rex to take over for him.

"I came back to see how the research was going," I said. "What's happened?"

He leaned over to speak quietly, although whatever it was he had to tell me I doubted it was a secret anymore. "Kenneth fell down the stairs. Hit his head."

I peered up at him in question, waiting for him to finish.

"He's dead," he whispered.

A shadow loomed in the glow from the outside lights. "Now you're even beating me to the scene," Detective Jackson's familiar deep voice drawled from behind.

Jamie straightened and spotted the shiny badge on Jackson's belt. "They certainly have sent a lot of people out to an accidental fall," Jamie said brusquely.

Jackson nodded. "We like to be thorough. If you don't mind, I'd like to borrow Miss Taylor for a moment." He took hold of my elbow and moved me along. "Bluebird, why are you always around when people end up dead?"

I stopped and pulled my arm free from his grasp. "Maybe I'm just a really good journalist." I squeezed a grin at him.

"Or maybe you're just drawn to trouble." He motioned for me to follow him.

Three medics were huddled around the last few steps on the staircase, the infamous stairs where Lauren Grace met her tragic end. Blood smears stained the floral wallpaper lining the walls along the staircase. Dark stains marred the oak banister as well. It seemed it had been quite a violent tumble.

One of Kenneth's black leather loafers was sitting on the second from the top step. The other one was still on his foot. From my vantage point, with the shield of medics surrounding him, I could only see his trousers and feet. His legs were splayed at odd angles as if he had died quickly from a blow to the head and then bounced down the rest of the stairs like a rag doll.

A medic, a young woman with tattoos on her neck, heard us approach. "Detective Jackson, we need you to second our opinion that the victim is deceased." She stood up, revealing the rest of the grisly scene.

Kenneth Applegate's head was in a pool of blood. His mouth was open wide as if he'd been frightened before falling, but that was probably just the natural reaction of someone who had passed the point of no return in a fall down a flight of stairs. Blood coated his beard and glued his hair to his forehead. He must have sustained a violent blow to the head on his way down.

Detective Jackson pulled on a glove and performed the unpleasant task of feeling for a pulse. Although he wasn't the last word, a doctor was required for that, he had the authority to call the coroner to the scene. He removed the glove he was wearing and dropped it into the biological waste container the medics had carried inside. He nodded to let me know he was dead and pulled out his phone to call the coroner.

A tiny voice squeaked behind me. "Psst, Miss Taylor."

I turned around to find Kitty Bloomfield hiding behind the edge of the doorway. It seemed, rather than hiding from the tragic sight on her staircase, she was trying to avoid seeing what was going on. I couldn't blame her. Death was never something anyone was anxious to see, and poor Mr. Applegate had had a terrible and messy accident.

Kitty's pinkish-blonde pile of curls was drooping down the side of her head and several hairpins were sticking out. She was pale white with worry. I could only imagine the terror and confusion in her home when this all took place.

I walked over and immediately grabbed hold of her shaky hands. "How are you doing, Kitty?"

"Not so good. I don't understand how it happened but then I suppose it wasn't the first time someone fell and died on those stairs."

I creased my brow in question.

"Lauren Grace," she whispered. "Which brings me to something important." She looked past me to Detective Jackson. He was checking out the banister and stairs. "I noticed you were friendly with that nice looking policeman. He's not in uniform. Is he a detective?"

"Yes, I'm sure he was called only because the accident resulted in death."

She pulled out a linen, embroidered handkerchief from the pocket of her sweater and wiped her brow. "Yes. But I should talk to him."

"Yes, of course. Did you witness Mr. Applegate's fall?"

She shook her head and one of the dangling hairpins came loose. I pulled it the rest of the way out and handed it to her. She quickly jammed it right back into her pile of curls. "I didn't witness it. I don't believe there was anyone with Mr. Applegate when he fell, but Wilma pulled me aside a few minutes ago. She's quite shaken." She looked past me again to Detective Jackson. "She really should talk to the detective. I don't want to mess things up by trying to retell what she heard."

Jackson just happened to glance our way. I waved him over. He said something to the medics and joined Kitty and me at the doorway.

"Detective Jackson, this is Kitty Bloomfield. She owns the Dandelion Inn." I turned to Kitty. "Kitty, this is Detective Jackson."

She smiled demurely up at him. "Oh my, you're tall."

"Kitty, you mentioned something about Wilma," I reminded her before she floated off in a school girl blush-worthy daydream.

"Yes," she cleared her throat. "Detective Jackson, I think you should come have a talk with my housekeeper. She's quite shaken about something she heard just before Mr. Applegate fell."

"Of course. Can you lead me to her?" Jackson asked.

"Right this way."

We followed Kitty into the dining room. Lauren Grace, with her ethereal smile, gazed down at the room from her gilt frame over the mantel. Both Wilma and Lucy, the chef, were sitting at the table, clutching glasses of water and seemingly consoling each other.

"Wilma, this is Detective Jackson," Kitty said as we entered. "Why don't you tell him what you told me."

Wilma looked at Lucy. They both exchanged nods. Wilma turned back to us. "It wasn't just me. Turns out Lucy was in this room and heard the same thing I heard from the parlor." She stared up at Detective Jackson. "That man didn't just fall," Wilma said. "Someone or something pushed him."

CHAPTER 20

*A*fter a shocking revelation by two members of the staff and apparent witnesses, the tragic scene took on a whole new slant. Detective Jackson made the decision to not ask any questions while the two women sat together in the dining room and instead opted for a private conversation with each before talking to the other guests. Being mid-week and off season, aside from Kitty and her two live-in staff members, the only other people in the house were the APPS visitors. Jackson asked them to gather in the sitting room at the opposite end of the house, so he could talk with them. But the coroner's arrival had stalled the interviews.

Jackson had gone off to talk with the coroner while I helped a very shaken Kitty prepare a tray of coffee. It seemed it would be a long night. Angela and Barbara had both asked for theirs to be laced with whiskey. I couldn't blame either of them. Their ghost adventure had turned into a true horror movie. Especially if Wilma and Lucy's assertions that Kenneth was pushed were correct.

Since Kitty and I were the only people in the kitchen, I decided to ask a few questions to clarify the night's events. "Kitty, where were the other guests when the accident happened?"

"Let me think back. It seems so long ago already." She dug her copper scoop into the coffee can. Her hands were trembling enough to dislodge some of the coffee onto the tile floor. It fell and spread out like tiny brown bugs. "Oh dear, I'm afraid this has been too overwhelming for me."

I reached for the coffee scoop before she spilled the rest of it. I patted her arm. "You sit over there on the chef's stool, and I'll make the coffee."

I led her to Lucy's leather topped stool positioned right in front of a desk with recipe notes and ingredient lists. I returned to my coffee making task.

I was about to prod Kitty along on my question when she started her response. "The guests, Mr. Applegate included, had gone to their rooms after dinner and dessert. They planned to rest and then meet downstairs in the parlor for a late evening excursion through the house. They were hoping Lauren Grace would make an appearance."

"So everyone was in their room when the accident happened?" I was still calling it an accident since nothing definitive had been decided yet. The word *murder* would only upset Kitty more. The whole thing was not just a terrible tragedy but a calamity for her business.

"As far as I know." She rubbed her hands together as if they were cold. "I was outside, in the carriage house, ironing linens when I heard Lucy scream. I rushed inside and found Lucy on the phone calling for paramedics." Kitty rubbed her forehead and paused to collect herself.

I crouched down with a wet paper towel and wiped the coffee grounds from the floor. Something occurred to me as I stood.

"Kitty, I don't want to upset you more, but if I could ask one more thing."

"Yes?"

"Kenneth had fallen across the bottom steps. How did everyone get downstairs?"

"When I arrived at the stairs, the guests were gathered at the top, staring down at the horrible scene below. Angela was scream-ing, and the men were trying to keep her from falling or slipping on the—blood." Her face blanched white at the word. I quickly got her a cup of water.

She took only a few sips and handed it back to me. "Anyhow, Lucy gave them directions to the servant stairs." Kitty tottered a second as she got up from the stool. She walked over to the butler's pantry and opened the door. "The servant stairs come out through the pantry."

I walked over and glanced inside. Just past the last set of shelves was a narrow door.

"For insurance purposes, I never allow guests to use that stair-well. It's dark and narrow. But tonight was an exception."

We stepped out from the pantry and found Detective Jackson just walking into the kitchen. "Miss Taylor, there you are. I'm going to interview Miss Acevado and Miss Knowles separately, and I need your assistance."

"I'm feeling a bit better, Sunni," Kitty said. "I'll finish the coffee."

"If you're sure," I said.

"Yes, I'm fine."

I followed Jackson out to the dining room. Wilma had stayed in the room waiting for her interview. Lucy had gone in to see that the guests were doing all right in the parlor.

Jackson lowered his voice. "There weren't any female officers on duty, and I thought the women would be more comfortable with you in the room."

"Absolutely."

Wilma was sitting on the settee at the side of the room with her head resting back and her eyes closed. I hopped up on tiptoes to whisper. He pushed his long hair back and I got a slight whiff of his very pleasant aftershave. "What did the coroner say?"

"He says everything indicates death from head trauma. Now we just need to find out whether or not the fall was an accident or intentional."

I landed back on my heels. "Did you say 'we'?" I asked enthusiastically.

"Actually, I meant the law enforcement team, but I suppose one industrious journalist can be part of that 'we'. Why were you here anyhow?"

"I'm doing a story on the Applegate Society. Or at least I was."

"Always on top of the story before it even happens," he quipped. "Let's go see if this was just an accident. Although something tells me, since you're involved, it's not going to be that simple."

"Not sure how to take that," I muttered behind him as we approached Wilma.

"Miss Knowles," Jackson said in a low, smooth voice that would catch even a sleeping woman's attention. (It certainly caught mine.) Wilma had an old fashioned name, but she looked anything except out of date. She had a diamond stud in her nose and a pair of silver skull earrings. Her face gained instant color when she saw who was standing over her.

"I'm sorry. I dozed off." She smoothed her hair back and sat up straighter on the settee. "Are you ready for my statement?"

"Yes, if you don't mind." Jackson swung two chairs around from a nearby table and motioned for me to sit. Wilma smiled weakly at me.

"I've asked Miss Taylor to join us," Jackson said. "She is a journalist for the *Junction Times*, but your statement is not for the paper." He shot me an admonishing glance to make sure I understood. Which I did. I was hardly the type of journalist to parse out wild accusations and rumors.

"I'm just trying to assess what happened here tonight," Jackson continued. "First, can you tell me where you were and what you were doing when Mr. Applegate fell?"

It was only the first question and Wilma was already fidgeting with the hem on her shirt. "I was in the parlor dusting the furniture."

"Seems a little late for housecleaning chores," Jackson said.

She lowered her voice, even though we were alone in the room. "Kitty Bloomfield is obsessive about dust and cleanliness. The guests had spent some time in there after dinner. I knew Kitty would lecture me if I didn't have the room spotless in the morning. I have to work hard here, but my room and food are free and she pays well. She can't help herself about the dust. She likes the place spotless."

"So you were alone in the parlor dusting furniture?" he asked.

"Yes. Just me and my dust cloth." She flashed him an unnecessary smile. I wondered how many of those the man received in an average day.

"What happened next?" Jackson wasn't taking notes. For the time being, it was just an accidental fall.

"I was polishing the brass sconces on the wall when I heard some footsteps coming from upstairs. A few seconds later, I heard a man say 'no, please'. It was quiet, and I almost thought I'd imagined it. Then his voice grew louder, more agitated. He said—" Wilma lifted her eyes to remember the exact words. "'No, don't. Get away. Go away.' Then there was a series of thumping sounds and some terrible cracking noises and a groan. A few seconds later, Lucy was screaming."

"Did you hear anyone answer him or threaten him as he pleaded to be left alone?"

She chewed her bottom lip in thought. "Hmm, not that I can remember. I just heard him."

"What did you do then?"

"I raced out to see if I could help." She shrugged her shoulders weakly. "There was nothing to do. Anyone who's ever watched one of those doctor or emergency room shows could see the man was dead."

"Thank you for your time. Did you say Miss Acevado was with the guests in the parlor?"

"I'll go check for you," I said. The coroner's team had set up several white screens, like something a photographer might use, to keep the scene from view. A gurney sat halfway through the entryway, waiting to carry off Mr. Applegate. Wilma's retell of the events before his fall were certainly distressing. It seemed as if he was almost fighting someone off at the top of the stairs.

Lucy was helping Kitty pass out coffees when I reached the parlor. Angela spotted me and nearly spilled her coffee. "What is happening? Where is Detective Jackson? I need to know what is going on." Her face was pinched and red and her eyes swollen. Barbara sat quiet and still as a statue in one of the upholstered chairs near the window. She stared out into the darkness as if lost. This had to be a heartbreaking shock for the woman. It was so clear to see that she simply adored the man. In fact, one might even say she was as obsessed with Kenneth as he was obsessed with the ghost of Lauren Grace.

"I think Detective Jackson will be talking to you shortly," I said. "Miss Acevado, you're needed in the dining room."

"Right." Lucy handed a cup of coffee to Rex. He looked considerably less upset than his female counterparts. Of course, he wasn't a sibling or an adoring fan, so that made some sense. Jamie also didn't look too put out by it all. He'd set up his laptop and a few of his ghost detection devices on the roll top desk in the corner of the room.

Lucy and I walked back through to the dining room. "Detective Jackson wants to ask you a few questions. He's asked me to sit in on the interviews with women because there are no female officers on site."

"I'm sure that's protocol," Lucy said. She didn't seem to mind me sitting in.

Jackson was recording a few notes on his phone as we stepped into the room. He slipped his phone back into his pocket and motioned for Lucy to sit on the settee.

"It's been a long night so I'll get straight to it, Miss Acevado, if you don't mind."

"Not at all," Lucy said and settled back. She was much calmer than Wilma.

"Where were you when Mr. Applegate fell?"

"Why, I was right here in this room. I was putting serving dishes back in the buffet. Kitty likes things to be stacked neatly, so it takes me some time to do it just right."

"Yes, I'm gathering that Miss Bloomfield is very particular about her inn," Jackson said.

Lucy sighed loudly. "I'm sure it hasn't really set in for her yet. The staircase—it's such a mess."

"Right." Jackson was taken aback by her mention of the mess on the stairs, but his reaction was subtle enough that Lucy didn't notice or bother to apologize for the crass remark. "We have special crews that can help with that," he added. "Back to those final moments. You were here stacking dishes. What happened next?"

"I was humming to myself, a habit I can never seem to kick," she said with a chuckle. "Anyhow, over the sound of my hums, I heard a man say 'no don't, get away, go away'. Just a second or two later, I heard several loud thuds. My mind told me I was hearing a body thumping down the stairs, but I refused to believe it. I took a deep breath and raced out to see what had happened. Mr. Applegate's limp body was splayed on the bottom steps with his head covered in blood. I pulled out my phone to call for a paramedic." She fingered the collar of her shirt. "But I could tell he was gone. He wasn't moving at all."

"Was there anyone else there? On the stairs?"

"No, not until I screamed." She patted her chest. "I'm not usually prone to hysterics, but it was such a frightening scene."

Jackson nodded. "Yes, most people would have had the same reaction. Thanks for your statement. You can join the others in the parlor."

Lucy seemed disappointed to be dismissed so quickly. She walked out. Jackson pulled out his phone and made a call. "Hey, Everett, it's Jackson. Get some evidence bags out of the car. This just got moved from accidental death to possible murder."

CHAPTER 21

Following the same protocol, Jackson asked me to sit down with him when he briefly interviewed Angela on her whereabouts during the crucial moments before and after the fall. She was reasonably shaken and was only just starting to calm herself down from the shock of it. She'd remained in the parlor while everyone else had cleared out to the dining room.

"I was napping in my room," she said hoarsely. Her throat was strained from crying. "The chef's scream woke me from a dream." She rubbed her temple. "I can't remember what it was about, but the scream became part of the dream. Then I woke with a start. I quickly pulled on my shoes and headed out to the hallway to find out what was going on." She covered her face and her shoulders shook. "Can't believe it," she muttered into her hands.

"Do you need any assistance informing next of kin?" Detective Jackson asked. "We can provide you with that help if you need it."

She shook her face and lowered her hands. "I'm Ken's only remaining close family. Our father died ten years ago of a heart attack. Ken and I have different mothers. His was out of the picture before he was out of diapers. My mother didn't really get along with Ken, but I've left her a voice message. There are some distant cousins to call but that can wait. I'm going to need some time to process all this." Her voice wavered.

"Of course," Jackson said. "Let us know if we can help. Just a couple more questions—when was the last time you saw your brother alive?"

She pulled her sweater closer around her. "Must have been around eight this evening. We finished dinner and agreed to meet at ten in the drawing room for tonight's activity." She pulled a tissue out of her sleeve and wiped her nose. "Kenneth was looking so forward to it. He was sure we'd see the ghost of Lauren Grace during this stay."

Jackson looked at me. I winked to let him know I'd fill him in on ghost details later.

Jackson returned his attention to Angela. I sensed his hesitation and predicted what might be coming next. "Can anyone else confirm that you were in your room during the time between leaving the group and Kenneth's fall?"

Her swollen eyes rounded. "Confirm? No, of course not. I was alone. As I said, I was taking a nap. I don't understand the reasoning behind these questions. I thought it was an accident." She sat forward. "Is there something you're not telling me?"

"No, nothing is definite. There were a few witnesses who heard your brother speaking to someone just before he fell."

Angela covered her mouth. If she had been the murderer, she was doing an admirable job of looking stunned. "That's impossible. Everyone admired my brother. The witnesses must have been mistaken."

"I've no doubt of that. We're just being thorough."

"When will they take Kenneth out of the house? It seems like it's taking awfully long to move him." She whimpered a moment. "He needs to be taken off those horrible stairs. They are obviously dangerous. I'm sure that's why Lauren Grace fell to her death too. They are too slippery and too steep."

"I think the coroner is just getting ready to move Kenneth. I'll tell his assistant to let you know when they are closer." Jackson stood up. "Again, I'm sorry for your loss."

"Is there anything else I can get you, Angela?" I asked.

"No, thank you, Sunni. I'll just wait here until they need me. I have a great deal of thinking to do."

"Of course. I'll let you alone then." I followed Jackson out.

I had to speed up my pace to keep up with his long legs. The evidence crew was finished and just packing up their equipment. Jackson stopped to talk to them, while I continued on to the dining room.

Rex was sitting alone at one of the tables sipping a glass of what appeared to be whiskey. "Where's everyone else?" I asked.

"Barbara was feeling faint. Kitty helped her up the servant's stairs to her room. Nielsen? Who knows where that guy is. He's always up to his own thing. Never really wanted to be part of this group anyhow. He thinks we're all amateurs. Ken, included. They were constantly competing, but if you ask me, neither of them had much talent. Not that I often talk ill about the dead, but Kenny was more of a showman than a paranormal expert."

I sat down across from him. "And you? Are you one of those people gifted with extra sensory perception?"

"It comes and goes. But if you ask me—the ghost who haunts this inn most likely gave Kenny a push down those stairs."

It certainly wasn't what I expected Rex to say after the phrase 'if you ask me'. He was still wearing his corduroy professor coat with the elbow patches. The lingering scent of cigar assured me he'd stepped outside to have a smoke recently.

I took a long look at Lauren's portrait. Her smile was mild and serene, as if she was unhappy when the portrait was painted. "Why do you think Lauren Grace caused Ken to fall?"

Rex picked up his drink and swirled the amber liquid around before shooting it back. He finished the swallow with a satisfied sigh. "Kenneth was obsessed with Lauren Grace. It was like nothing I've ever seen before. Carried her picture in his wallet like she was alive and his wife. And he spent most of his time here staring at the portrait. When he wasn't staring at it, he was pestering Kitty for information. Where did she sleep? Were there any linens or personal items still in the house? Did Lauren Grace eat off the fine china stored in the buffet? He was obsessed with her. Any woman would have had more than enough."

"Yes but Lauren Grace is no longer alive." It seemed necessary to remind Rex.

"Obviously but these spirits can get angry just like the rest of us." He sat up straight and pulled a cigar out of his pocket. "That's my theory anyhow. If you don't mind, I need to go outside and have a chat with this cigar."

As he walked out, I mulled over his theory. I certainly knew that ghosts were capable of abrupt mood changes. That thought caused a short laugh to spurt from my lips. Was it possible that Lauren materialized just to scare the man who'd been staring at her portrait all day? It was an entirely ridiculous idea, and yet, it seemed Kenneth had definitely encountered someone on the stairs. And that *someone* was the last person to see him alive.

CHAPTER 22

*M*ost of the chaos had cleared. The coroner had taken Kenneth Applegate away. Plastic had been placed over the stairs until a crew could come in the morning to remove the blood. Everyone had gone to bed, although I doubted there would be much sleep.

Jackson finished talking to Kitty, letting her know what to expect for the next few days. He told her he'd be back in the morning to talk to the rest of the guests. She looked weary. It seemed she had hours ago given up the fight to keep her curls piled on top of her head. Her blondish-pink hair hung around her thin shoulders in complete disarray, giving her an almost childish quality.

I waited on the porch for Jackson. It was two in the morning, which meant I wouldn't be in bed until three at the earliest. The earlier adrenaline from discovering that Kenneth was dead had drained away leaving behind a heaviness that weighed down my limbs. I couldn't wait to flop down on my bed.

I rested my hands on the porch railing and gazed out at the

darkness. Birch Highlands, where Dandelion Inn was located, was a rustic mix of forest and open space. The vacant lot across the street was filled with tall weeds and the leftover wildflowers from summer.

Jackson walked out the front door. Kitty latched the door behind him. He had to be as tired as the rest of us but somehow he looked fresh, as if he'd just gotten out of bed.

"Do you have some sort of elixir at home that allows you to look like this after a long, grueling night?" I waved my arm up and down in front of him, but even that took too much effort. My hand flopped to my side.

Jackson smiled. "Come on, sleepyhead, let's get you to your jeep."

I trudged along next to him with invisible weights on my shoes. "Or maybe you're up late like this so often, you know, with your many *friends*, that staying up past midnight is just another day at the office." I covered my mouth. "Sorry, sleepiness has the same effect on me as four glasses of wine. Stuff just slips out of this mouth, and there's no reasonable thought behind it. So ignore me." I stopped abruptly. "Is she your girlfriend?"

His amber eyes looked wolfish under the late night moon. "Who?"

"The pretty redhead at the coffee shop." We started walking again. Rustling sounds in the brush landscape lining the road followed us to my jeep and caused me to walk a bit closer to Jackson.

"Just a friend who happens to be a girl," he said.

"Now I'm confused." I shook my head. "See lack of sleep makes me bubble headed."

"I don't know. You handled yourself pretty well in an ugly situation back there. Thanks for your help tonight."

"You're welcome." We reached the jeep. I turned to him. His hair ruffled just enough in the breeze to make it look like he was standing for a magazine shoot. "You know how much I enjoy a murder mystery."

"If that's what this is," he said. "Aside from the staff, the guests were all in their individual rooms, either resting or working on the computer. Which means no one can confirm anyone else's alibi."

"Did your team find anything of interest?"

"They took blood and tissue samples off various parts of the staircase. From a visual inspection, it seems he struck his head on the fourth oak balustrade. It's carved with a lot of corners." He reached into his pocket and pulled out a small evidence bag. "I did an inspection of my own at the top of the stairs and found this."

He held it up and shined his phone light through the bag. I squinted into the brightness. One long strand of yellow fiber or hair was curled up at the bottom of the bag.

"Is that a hair?" I asked.

"Didn't feel like it when I picked it up. I think it's nylon. Anyway, it might not have anything to do with the case."

"I don't know about that. I'm sure you gathered by the end of the night that the owner, Kitty Bloomfield, is very compulsive about cleanliness."

"I did and I can tell she's close to falling apart when she thinks about those stairs." He stuck the bag back into his pocket.

"I spent some time with everyone, Kenneth included, at my inn last night. I can tell you a few things I noted about the group's dynamics. I was in my journalist observation mode, so I've got it all up here." I tapped my temple.

"You're not too tired?"

"I passed tired two hours ago. I'm at that stage my mom used to call 'mild hysteria' where reality and fantasy and grumpiness collide. Her words, not mine. My dad, Pops, as we called him, loved to watch old movies late at night and I'd sneak out to watch with him occasionally. We kept it a secret from my mom, but she always knew because of 'mild hysteria'."

"Are you still close with your parents?" he asked.

Tired also tended to push my emotions into overdrive. The brief memory of watching television with my dad made my throat tighten. "I talk to my mom quite often." I swallowed before saying the sentence I always hated to say aloud. "Pops died of a heart attack while I was away at college. We were very close. He loved sports, and I was the family athlete."

"I'm sorry to hear that."

"Thanks. It gets a little easier each year, but that whole saying of 'time healing pain' should be revised to 'lots and lots of time heals pain.'"

Without warning, Jackson reached up and brushed a stray hair behind my ear. The simple, sweet gesture had a sobering effect . . . on both of us. A moment of awkward silence followed. It seemed he hadn't expected to do it any more than I'd expected it to happen.

"You should probably get home," he finally said to break the quiet. "Are you all right driving by yourself, or do you need a police escort?"

"I think I can make the short journey to Cider Ridge without getting lost. Thanks."

He reached to open the driver's side door.

"Wait, I was going to list a couple things I noticed about group dynamics," I said. "They might help you if this is a true murder case."

"It's late, Bluebird. Get some rest."

I stopped before sliding into the seat. "I can do quick bullet points." I held up my fingers and folded one with each observation. "Barbara Simpson was in love with Kenneth. Kenneth was obsessed with the ghost of Lauren Grace. Jamie Nielsen was always butting heads with Kenneth. Kenneth wrote a nasty review about Nielsen's book." I was down to my thumb. "Angela and Rex —hmm—I don't have too much to add about them. Although Rex did theorize this evening that the ghost of Lauren Grace had had enough of Kenneth staring at her portrait so she pushed him down the stairs."

"Good night, Bluebird."

"Good night, Detective Jackson."

CHAPTER 23

$\mathcal{L}$ ana and Raine were at my back door at what felt like the crack of dawn. It was ten in the morning. I climbed out of bed and pulled on my robe. Redford and Newman were sitting behind empty food bowls giving me doggie looks of disgust as I shuffled past them to the back door. I unlocked it and turned right around to make a beeline for the coffee pot.

"What have you done this time, little sister?" Lana said dejectedly as she followed Raine into the kitchen.

My head was still groggy and her accusation confused me. "Uh, I overslept because I was out late. It's hardly worth a lecture."

"I'm not talking about oversleeping and you know it." Lana sat on a stool and started peeling a banana.

I pulled the coffee can down from the cupboard. Redford barked sharply once, reminding me about their breakfast. I hurried over to the pantry to get a scoop of dog food.

For some inexplicable reason, Raine had wandered out of the kitchen into the rest of the house.

"Where's your electrician?" Lana asked as she broke off the tip of banana.

"He was driving out to the city this morning to pick up some parts. Thankfully. I had a long night, and I was just as glad not to have to wake early to let him inside."

Lana wiggled her bottom on the chair. "So glad that worked out for you, but why on earth did you have to kill off one of the society members? And the namesake one with all the decision power to boot."

I finished with the coffee and walked to the refrigerator for some orange juice. "Why would you say I killed him?"

"Because when my little sister shows up to a place, chaos is sure to follow."

I held up the orange juice. She shook her head. "One serving of fruit is more than enough this morning. What happened at Dandelion Inn? I heard Kenneth fell down the stairs. Did that Jamie guy finally get tired of their constant sniping and give him a push?"

My sister was not usually in such a surly mood. I was certain it had to do with her dream of hosting the paranormal convention falling tragically apart.

"Not sure how it happened yet." It wasn't my investigation to tell, so I kept any details, small as they were, out of the conversation.

"Maybe it was the ghost," Lana suggested. "They say she's a real pistol. Shows up at all hours of the night and even sometimes in the day. At least for those people who believe she exists." Lana was definitely not herself. I wondered if that was the reason for Raine disappearing the second they walked inside.

I walked to my kitchen cupboard. "Hey, sis, I've got your favorite cereal." I shook the box of Lucky Charms. "Those marshmallow rainbows will take that frown right off your face."

Lana signed loudly and put her elbows on the table. "Pour me a double. Lots of marshmallows, please, and plenty of luck to go with it because my own luck took a turn south."

I filled a bowl with cereal and milk and placed it down in front of her. "You don't know if the whole convention is cancelled. APPS is just a small group."

"But Kenneth Applegate is like the Grand Poobah of the whole big conglomeration of ghost enthusiasts. He was supposed to make the decision next week." She circled her spoon around the bowl of cereal, hunting for marshmallows. She caught a few and pushed them into her mouth. "Hmm, good stuff." She lowered the spoon into the bowl and her shoulders sank. "I had so many cool ideas for decorations and food. It was going to be a real *howling* event." She laughed at her play on words.

"Actually howling would be for a werewolf convention. Ghosts are more into moans and chain rattling."

"There you go stereo-typing incorporeal beings again," Raine said as she strode into the kitchen from the hallway.

"You're right. I think we have Charles Dickens to blame for the chain rattling thing." I lifted the box of cereal. "Lucky Charms?"

"No, thanks." Raine paced a few times in front of the hearth. Her brows were furrowed, and she fidgeted with the silver bangles on her wrist as if deep in thought.

I cocked a questioning brow at Lana. My forty-year-old sister was too busy chasing a yellow moon marshmallow around her bowl of milk.

"What are you doing, Raine?" I walked to the coffee maker.

She shook her head and muttered something, completely ignoring my question.

I filled a cup with coffee, walked over and ran the cup past her nose as she stared at the brick hearth.

She turned her face to me and adjusted her glasses. "For me?"

"Well, I wasn't trying to catch nose hairs for my coffee."

She took the cup and had a sip.

"Now that you've had some, why on earth are you pacing in front of my kitchen hearth?"

Her answer was apparently a half cup kind of response. She took a few more longer sips. "I felt something when I walked in here this morning." She leaned toward me to whisper. "I think he's upset about something."

I looked over at the dogs. They had already plowed through their food and were finding the best spots on their pillows for a morning nap.

"Not the dogs," she said louder. "Him. The ghost. I felt his presence last night when we were eating pizza. I didn't say anything because I knew I'd just get that—" She pointed at my face.

"What? My face. I can't really do anything about it. It's attached."

"No, see that. The mocking. I knew you wouldn't believe me just like I know you'll poo poo the feelings I'm having right now." She lifted her shoulders up and down. "I just can't shake it. Something about the aura in the house is different. It's darker, gloomier."

More and more, I was becoming a firm believer in Raine's psychic skills. In summer, she had predicted a murder that she couldn't possible have known anything about, and now it seemed she knew Edward was upset. Which he certainly was, even though he hadn't made an appearance all morning. Another sign that he wasn't himself.

"No mockery from me, Raine. If you're feeling it, then it must be true."

Lana had gotten wind of the conversation and was giving me a conspiratorial wink. I didn't return one. I would have been a terrible hypocrite to pretend I didn't believe Raine. Especially when I knew she was right.

"I've got to shower and get ready to start my day," I said.

Lana glanced at her phone. "At ten thirty in the morning. It'll be time for a lunch break as soon as you get to the newspaper office."

"Said the woman playing with her bowl of Lucky Charms," I said dryly. "Besides, I already texted Myrna to let her know I probably wouldn't be into the office today. It seems my pleasant, glowing article on the Applegate Society just took a very dark turn. I've got to regroup and find out the best way to approach it. I don't want to upset the group in case there is still a chance that the convention might end up here in Firefly Junction."

"Sure, throw in that little nugget to get a girl's hopes up," Lana said.

"Oh snap out of it, Lana," Raine said sharply. "You've been moping all morning. It'll all work out fine. Besides you already have two fall wedding receptions planned for late October. It's not like you'll be sitting idly by the phone waiting for them to call." Sometimes Raine was better at handling my sister than me. I was unfortunately always stuck in that little sister status. After years of childhood together, our sibling hierarchy was pretty much cemented in stone. Raine got to come in from a coworker's angle, and that was what Lana needed this morning.

Lana got up from the stool and carried her bowl to the sink. "You're right, Raine. You must be psychic or something." She added that dig just to keep things in check. She was after all older than Raine and her boss. "Let's go to the barn and start working out the decoration list for the Olson wedding."

"Yes, good idea," I said. "I've procrastinated long enough. I need to shower and get going." I suddenly had an urge to find out more about Bonnie Ross, the woman who had very possibly raised Edward's child. My few months at the *Junction Times* had already given me some good contacts for town records and historical data. I knew exactly the place to start.

CHAPTER 24

*T*he city hall, or municipal building as some people called it, was just over Colonial Bridge at the front edge of the Birch Highlands turnoff. Since Firefly Junction was a central town in the middle of four small towns, the city hall functioned for all four. The month before, I'd been assigned an article on the rejuvenation project at the local cemetery in Smithville. Part of the assignment required me to do research on some of the older graves, ones that had stone markers so worn from time and weather, the names could no longer be read. That part of the research had taken me to city hall, and more specifically, the records office. And even more specifically, Orson Nettles, the record keeper.

I walked through the lobby of the building. The entire place had been painted in a dull yellow. Wood paneling ran along the bottom half of the walls, signaling that the place had not had a facelift in many years. Even the fake ferns next to the elevators looked like plants out of the Jurassic period.

The elevator pinged and the doors slid open. I tapped my foot to the equally outdated music and briefly wondered what was happening at Dandelion Inn. I didn't want to be pushy, but it seemed I had every right to show up and find out what was going on. I'd been part of the entire ordeal, after all.

I reached the floor for the records office and quickly tried to narrow down exactly what I was looking for. It made sense to start right at the source, in this case, Bonnie Ross. It seemed plausible that I'd find a marriage certificate and that would lead me to Bonnie's maiden name.

I opened the door to the records office. Three blue upholstered chairs sat along a wall with a hand-painted map of Firefly Junction and the surrounding towns. The chairs were empty which was a good sign . . . for me. It meant no one was waiting.

I rang the bell on the front counter and bit my lip to hold back an amused smile as I waited for Orson to come around the corner. His shoes shuffled over the tile floor of the hallway before he stepped around the doorway into the front office. Orson was a well past middle aged guy with tufts of dark gray hair and amazingly glowing skin, as if he exfoliated every day. He was wearing the exact same shamrock green sweater. His nametag declaring him the Records Clerk was sewn onto the sweater. But the thing that stood out more starkly about Orson than anything else was that he moved like a sloth . . . literally. (Although, maybe not, since sloths are not bipedal.) But Orson moved his limbs with fluid grace and careful purpose and always in slow motion. It was as interesting as it was aggravating to watch. Especially when you needed him to find a record and his journey to the file cabinets took an hour.

"Miss Taylor, correct?" Apparently, his memory was much faster than his body.

"Yes, hello, Mr. Nettles. It's nice to see you again."

He still hadn't quite made it to the counter. I wanted to reach forward, grab the sides of his sweater and give him a little tug.

Instead of that rudeness, I concluded I didn't necessarily need him to reach the counter to ask the question. Only, he tossed his out first.

"More research for the *Junction Times*? I thought you did a swell job on that article about the cemetery. And thank you for mentioning my name. I showed it to my mom and she got a kick out of seeing my name in the paper."

"Of course. You were a great help. I'm glad it made your mom happy." I briefly let my mind wander to what a Mrs. Nettles was like and if she moved any faster than her son. And just how old was the woman? Maybe tortoises had it right. Maybe slow movement was the secret to long life. Ugh, silly tangent. "Actually, I'm doing some research on Cider Ridge Inn."

He finally reached his destination, the front counter. Even creasing his forehead in question took longer than normal. "That old place? I thought they'd be tearing that thing down soon."

I cleared my throat. "No, I don't think so. It's going to be renovated."

"Really? Are you sure?"

"Yes, I think so. I know the owner well. What I was wondering —is there any way to get a copy of the original owner's marriage certificate? A man named Cleveland Ross built the place for his bride. I think they were married in the first decade of the nineteenth century."

"Yes, I know about Cleveland Ross." He scooted slowly to the notepad and pen and pulled them closer. With painstaking precision he wrote the name Cleveland Ross on the notepad. I could only figure he needed to write the name down in case he forgot it during the long journey to the file cabinets. With equal care and precision, he added the letter MC to the note, which I could only guess meant marriage certificate.

"For the old records, I need to go to the file cabinets in the back room. The city hired someone to scan the old records into the computer, a high school kid," he said with some derision. "He spent so much time on his phone, while he was supposed to be working, I'm surprised he got as a far as he did." He paused. Naturally, his pauses were longer than the conventional pause. "1900," he said finally.

"1900?" I asked. He'd lost me during the long interlude.

"That's how far he got when he wasn't on his phone," Orson grumbled. "Have a seat and I'll go look for this."

I gritted my teeth and fantasized about shoving roller skates on his feet as I watched him shuffle to the back room. This had probably been a mistake, but I didn't know how else to find out about Bonnie.

After fifteen minutes of catching up on emails and social media posts, Orson shuffled back out to the counter holding a folder.

"What did you find?"

He lifted the folder. "I've got something you might like to see." He continued his snail crawl to the counter. It seemed I would have to wait to know the contents of the folder once he landed at his final destination, the front counter. The oddest thing about Orson's slowness was there didn't seem to be any physical reason for it, no heavy breathing, no signs of a stroke or past injury. It seemed he just preferred not to rush.

He laid the folder on the counter with great ceremony as if he had uncovered the secrets to the construction of the pyramids. "Not only did I find the marriage certificate, but there was a birth certificate as well."

My feet did a shuffling happy dance. "Wonderful. You might have saved me an extra round of research. I'm interested in the birth of a baby."

Orson grinned as he turned the folder my direction. "Let me know if you need anything else. It's quiet in here today. I'm thinking I might use the spare time to reorganize my office space."

A flashing image of Orson carrying a single binder from one

shelf to another at his natural pace forced me to hold in a snicker. "Thank you, I'll let you know."

I opened the folder. Orson began the long, arduous ten foot journey to the hallway and his office. The marriage certificate had been slipped into clear plastic. The yellow parchment embossed with brown lettering declaring it a 'certificate of marriage' was in surprisingly excellent condition. The ink had faded some and the writing was in that stylish calligraphy of the time, but I could make out the important parts. Cleveland Richard Ross married Bonnie Louise Milton on the seventh day of June 1810.

I was anxious to get to the birth certificate. I pulled out the next plastic sleeve, and instantly, my enthusiasm deflated. The date on the certificate was April 4th, 1792. It couldn't possibly have been Bonnie's baby. Upon further reading, I discovered that I was holding Bonnie Louise Milton's birth certificate. Some quick math told me she was eighteen when she married Cleveland Ross. Bonnie was born in Boston and weighed five pounds at birth.

Orson shuffled back before he even reached his office. "I can make copies of those if you like. The copy machine is just down the hall."

"Uh no, that's all right." I want to be home in time for Christmas, I thought wryly. "Can I just take a piece of this notepad and write down the information?"

"Be a lot easier to copy them but suit yourself," he said and turned back around.

I quickly jotted down names and dates. It was a start. "Thanks again for all your help, Orson," I called.

"You're welcome."

I left the certificates in the folder on the counter and hurried out to the elevator. I'd wasted more than enough time today. I needed to find out what was going on with the Applegate Society. At this point, I had nothing for the paper, and Parker was never pleased when the story was late. I was no longer sure what angle to use.

I stepped out of the elevator. Just as I walked through the glass doors, an ambulance and paramedic raced by. I didn't think much about it until Detective Jackson's car trailed quickly behind the emergency vehicles. I ran for my jeep. I knew that where there was Jackson there was murder.

Or at the very least, trouble.

CHAPTER 25

Once again, there was a string of emergency vehicles in front of Dandelion Inn.

"Poor Kitty," I muttered as I parked the jeep past all the chaos. It was the same exact scene, only this time with the addition of sunlight. That aspect alone made it all seem less dire than the night before.

Jackson was already inside the house before I drove past. I raced up the porch steps and through the open front door. The biological hazard cleaning crew was still working on the main staircase. The entire area had been cornered off with cones and yellow tape and the crew worked behind a sheet of plastic.

The activity seemed to be centered around the drawing room. Angela and I ran into each other as I turned the corner of the hall-way. She dropped the phone she was just about to answer. It bounced behind me. I quickly turned around and picked it up. The call was from the Hamilton and Peterson Law Firm. I handed it back to her. She nodded a thank you and rushed past me to answer it. Whatever was happening in the drawing room wasn't bad enough to keep Angela from answering her phone. I wondered if she was already checking on her brother's estate. He was not even off the morgue table yet but then who was I to judge.

Jackson was chatting with a paramedic when I reached the room. He spotted me and winked but didn't stop the conversation. Barbara was sitting on a gurney looking pale and listless as one of the medics finished her vitals. Kitty was standing at the back of the room looking as if she just wanted to wake up from this bad dream.

I circled the activity and reached Kitty's side. "You look as if you could use a glass of water," I suggested.

"No, thank you, I'm fine." Her hands trembled as she pulled at the sides of her sweater. "I've never had such a terrible week."

"What happened to Barbara?"

"I found her in this room slumped on the couch like a rag doll. She could barely talk and was hyperventilating. Mumbling something about taking too many pills and not being able to go on without Kenny."

Right then, a paramedic walked into the room with a bottle of antacid. I turned my ear to hear the conversation with Detective Jackson.

"This is the only medication I could find in her room," the paramedic said.

Jackson took hold of the bottle and walked over to the gurney. "Miss Simpson, are these the pills you took?"

Barbara opened her eyes with a dramatic flutter. "Yes, at least ten. Maybe twelve she said weakly."

Jackson and the medics exchanged amused glances.

"All right, Miss Simpson," the medic said. "We're going to take you to the hospital, so the doctors can take a look at you."

Barbara relaxed back. She looked small and remarkably older resting on the gurney.

Kitty walked past me muttering something about needing a

vacation. I followed Jackson out to the front porch. There wasn't much need for a detective or a journalist at an accidental antacid overdose. Still, poor Barbara looked so distraught about Kenny, I was sure she'd suffer the heartbreak of his loss for a long time.

Jackson and I headed past the stairs and the clean-up crew. "I asked the group to stay in town an extra day until I had more information on Applegate's death. Maybe that was a mistake. At least for the women. They are both distraught."

"Well, you couldn't very well ask only the men to stay. After all, women are capable of murder too." I stopped our progress to the front porch where I saw Rex leaning on the railing smoking his pungent cigar. "Which reminds me—" I glanced around. With the exception of the ruckus on the stairs, we were alone. I turned back to Jackson. "This is probably completely irrelevant, but on the way into the drawing room just now, I ran smack dab into Angela. She was just about to answer her phone. Our accidental crash caused her to drop it. As I picked it up, I noticed the screen said Hamilton and Peterson Law Firm."

"Maybe she was checking on her brother's will," he suggested.

"My thought too only it seems a bit early to be thinking about that. And some previous research mentioned that Martin Applegate, their father, was heir to a large fortune, even though he lived frugally and spent most of his adult life traveling in a Volkswagen bus hunting for ghosts."

Jackson nodded. "Interesting. I'll check into it. Money is always the go-to motive for murder. Good thing I've always got a little bluebird twittering about murder scenes, looking for clues."

"And this time, I didn't even need to hide in a tree."

We walked out to the porch. A cluster of angry looking rain clouds had settled over the valley, and the air had that distinctive scent of precipitation. The medics were just loading Barbara into the ambulance. Angela had kindly volunteered to go with her. She climbed in behind the gurney. Rex watched the scene from the porch.

"That woman had herself so starry-eyed about Kenny, she's made herself sick over it." Cigar smoke trailed up from his nose as Rex spoke. The smell of the cigar was making my eyes water. "What did the coroner say?" Rex asked.

Jackson checked his phone. "Nothing yet but I expect to hear soon. Not sure if it'll tell us much anyhow. The blow to the head was severe enough to make it an obvious cause of death."

Rex blew out a smoke ring. "Like I said, I think that ghost had enough of Kenny fawning over her, staring at her painting, carrying the picture in his wallet. Those spirits can get pretty ornery when they're upset."

"Tell me about it," I grumbled before I could stop myself. I instantly had both men's undivided attention. "I mean, so I've heard. I heard they can get really—really—" I squinted at Rex. "What was the word you used?"

"Ornery," he coughed behind the word.

"Yes, ornery. That's what I've heard." Rex bought my stammering response, but Jackson already knew me too well. His perfectly shaped brow arched like a black rainbow. Fortunately, he let it go without further scrutiny.

He turned back to Rex. "Mr. Thunder, I know you're very dialed in to the spirit world, but I can't investigate a ghost. I'm going to have to stick with facts and people still of this world. I hope to let all of you go home tomorrow. I'm sorry for the inconvenience."

Jackson and I headed down the steps. "What's that saying?" Jackson muttered quietly. "Me thinks thou doth protest too much."

"Ooh, how Shakespearean of you," I quipped. "Although, I think the line was 'the lady doth protest too much, me thinks'."

"Yes, well, I tended to skip eleventh grade English class when the Shakespeare came out."

"I see. I suppose you were performing you own version of Romeo and Juliet somewhere behind the gymnasium instead."

He didn't shake his head to the contrary. "Let's just say I probably had way too much fun in high school."

We reached the jeep. Most of the emergency vehicles had pulled away, including the ambulance, but the whole scene was just too familiar. "Is this like that movie where the guy has to keep repeating the same day?" I asked. "I think we were standing right here in this spot." I tapped my driver side door. "And standing right next to this very cool jeep just twelve hours ago."

"You're right. Only you were wearing a blue coat and the loose strand of hair was on the right." He reached up and tucked a strand of hair back behind my left ear. The same awkward silence followed but the duration was shorter.

"What were you saying about Rex protesting too much?"

He glanced back at the house. Rex had gone inside. "It's nothing, I'm sure. It's just that sometimes when a person is guilty, they look for scapegoats and toss out other people's motives."

"Trying to throw you off the scent, eh? Although, it's hard to find any scent behind the noxious fumes of that cigar."

"Huh, I kind of liked the way it smelled. It reminded me of my Uncle Pete. Anyhow, I've got to get back to the station. Thanks for the tip on the phone call from the lawyer."

"You're welcome. And next time we meet, let's try a different location. You know, change things up a bit."

He laughed.

"Maybe without a murder victim too," I added.

"Good idea." He opened the door for me. "Actually, why don't I come by your house later with some dinner."

I very nearly fell back into the jeep as if a blast of air had hit me. "Dinner? Tonight?"

"It'll be my way to say thanks for helping out on these murder cases."

His explanation was slightly deflating, but it helped me gather my wits. It was just a thank you dinner, and nothing more. No date mentioned. I quickly chastised myself for immediately jumping to conclusions. This was much better. The last thing I needed was to date Detective Brady Jackson.

"I'd take you out properly, but I've got a ton of work to do at the office so it might be kind of late. Say eight? Do you like burgers and fries?"

"I never say no to burgers and fries." I marveled at how coolly I answered when my insides had gone to jelly.

"Great. I'll see you then."

CHAPTER 26

"It is just a thank you dinner, burger and fries in my own kitchen. Don't read too much into it," I told my reflection in the mirror as I checked my hair and outfit choice for the tenth time. My hair looked too brunette and my skin looked too olive tonight. How I wished I could occasionally borrow Emily's fairy princess coloring. "Argh," I growled. "There I go again making this a bigger deal than it is." I dragged myself away from the mirror and headed to the kitchen.

"Making what into a big deal?" Edward was leaning against the kitchen counter tossing Newman's ball in the air and making my dog crazy at the same time.

"If you're going to tease him with that ball, at least have the decency to throw it," I sniped.

I walked to the pantry to get some apples for the bowl on the table. It was always good to falsely display how healthy my eating habits normally were just before a burger and fries. As I reached for the pantry door, Newman's tennis ball whizzed past my ear and ricocheted like a stray bullet off the kitchen wall.

I spun around with nostrils flared.

Edward shrugged. "You said to throw it."

"So it's going to be one of those nights, eh? I haven't seen you for over a day and *now* you show up. And in an obnoxious mood, no less. Tonight of all nights." My chin nearly dropped to the floor. "Tonight of all nights," I repeated weakly. "How did I forget about my intrusive tenant when I said yes to dinner here?" The question was for me, but Edward chimed right in.

"I'm not your tenant. I'm just allowing you to live here," he corrected.

"Right, allowing me to pay for everything and make sure this place doesn't come down around your vaporous, yet amazingly supersonic, ears." A new question about Edward's existence popped into my head. "What would happen to you if this house was torn down?"

As usual his response was filled with sarcasm and no actual facts. "I can't tell because no one has torn it down yet. But with the way that human colossus has been tinkering with the switches and wires, we might soon find out. Only the explosion will save the work of tearing the place down."

"As usual, you exaggerate. Tom said he'd be done by next week. I hope my *landlord* can put up with the inconvenience just a bit longer."

"You sure are in a foul mood," he drawled.

I pointed to my chest. "I'm in a bad mood? Please. If we're going to compete for champion grump, you're already wearing the crown."

Newman returned the ball and dropped it in front of Edward. Edward blew the ball, and it rolled slowly across the kitchen floor. The dog still chased it exuberantly as if it had been thrown.

"*Who* is coming to dinner?" My silent wish that he wouldn't ask was dashed.

"Just a friend. And you will make yourself scarce. No wait, not scarce. Invisible. Extinct. What's a more exact word so there's no lack of interpretation? Gone. You just make sure you are gone from this general area and the entire downstairs. All right?"

"Is it a date?" He blew the ball harder. It rolled into the hallway. Newman skittered after it.

"No, no it's not a date. It's a thank you dinner." I slipped into the pantry and grabbed some apples from the shelf. I carried them out and arranged them in the ceramic bowl on the table.

"Maybe you should think about it," he suggested.

"Think about what?" I leaned back to admire my artistry. I was going for the casual yet organized apple bowl look.

Edward floated over to the table. "About going on a date. Might help your mood."

I blinked over at him. "Is there any chance your middle world eternity is going to end soon because I feel like I'm living with my mom right now. That reminds me. So much happened in the past few days, I forgot all about the records office." Surprisingly, he didn't interrupt so I continued. "I'm on a mission to find out what happened to your baby."

Just the mention of the baby caused his image to fade, his visual version of a mood change.

"No, don't disappear, Edward. At least not yet. Later, yes. Please."

That made him angry enough to come sharply back into focus.

"I think that's what's keeping you here. You don't know what happened to the baby and to future Edward Beckett generations." The pitter patter of raindrops drummed lightly on the roof.

"What if none of it is good news? Maybe it's better not to know." He drifted to the window.

"So that's why you're so bristly. You're worried you left behind a string of dissolute characters."

"How I miss the feel of rain on my skin." He gazed out the window a second longer. "Bristly? Sometimes you use the oddest phrases. And I'm not worried about my legacy. I was the dark horse of the Beckett family in England. And it suited me just fine."

"What is it then?"

He faded away and I thought he'd gone. I startled when he materialized right in front of me. "What if there was tragedy? What if Bonnie died in childbirth like so many women do?"

"Did," I corrected. "Medicine and maternal care have improved quite a bit since then. I think this will help you, Edward," I said with complete sincerity.

"Fine. Research away then. Just keep the undesirable stuff to yourself."

"Agreed. So far, nothing undesirable. I discovered Bonnie's maiden name."

"Milton," he said.

"Darn it. You already knew?"

"Of course. Why wouldn't I? Back then we talked to each other and wrote letters, unlike now when you communicate through little slabs of metal."

"I'll bet you didn't know that she was born—"

"In Boston," he said casually.

"Darn it again. Jeez, talk about having the wind taken out of my sails. I just spent a perfectly good morning watching a human-sized sloth shuffle around a hundred square foot office as if he was traversing the globe and all for not. I just needed to ask the ghost in the attic." I laughed. "I like that. The ghost in the attic. Could be book title."

A knock sent me straight to attention.

"By the way, that arrogant detective pulled up to the house while you were thinking up book titles and astounding me with all the momentous information you uncovered."

I smoothed my hair. "All right, that's your cue to fritter away and be gone. And behave."

"What is this word 'behave'?"

"Funny ghost. Now go away." I headed to the door with my heart doing just a bit too much dancing for a thank you dinner.

CHAPTER 27

*T*he pitter patter had turned instantly to a downpour. Jackson was wet and dripping (a look he managed to pull off just fine) as he stepped into the house.

He lifted his coat to reveal both his shoulder holster and the bag of food he had safely tucked away from the deluge. "Nothing worse than soggy burgers."

"Except soggy fries," I amended as I led him to the kitchen.

"See, I had you figured for a crispy fry girl. I asked for them to be well done."

Redford and Newman greeted him with extra exuberance. Jackson laughed when Redford nearly knocked him over. "I've got to stop wearing that cheeseburger cologne."

I grabbed two plates from the cupboard and set them on the pine table. "I hope you don't mind if we eat in the kitchen. The dining room isn't quite finished."

Jackson looked around the kitchen. "This room is bigger than my entire house." He placed the food on the table.

"Where do you live?"

"A little cabin in Hickory Flats."

"What would you like to drink?" I asked. "I've got soda, milk and orange juice."

He pulled the burgers out of the bag. "Water is fine."

I proceeded to fill up two glasses with ice water and tried to ignore the tiny tremble in my hands.

"Sorry I'm late, by the way," Jackson said as I carried the waters to the table. "It seemed like everyone and their second cousins needed to talk to me just as I headed for the door."

I sat down next to him and he slid my burger over.

"Dr. Fritz, the coroner, called to confirm that Kenneth died from a blow to the head. The tissue samples—" He stopped. "Way to go, Jax," he said to himself. "Tissue samples always make the best conversation starters at the dinner table."

I opened a pack of ketchup. "No, continue. I don't mind. I'm interested to hear."

He smiled just enough to make that finger tremble start again. "You are definitely not like other women, Bluebird."

I swirled the fry through the ketchup. "Is that a good thing or bad thing?"

"Good." He unwrapped his burger. "Anyhow, Fritz told me the tissue from the banister matched Applegate's. In fact all the tissue samples came from him. There was no glaring signs of foul play except, strangely enough, there was a pink bruise on his upper chest."

I sped up my swallow. "So maybe someone pushed him and left the mark on his chest."

"That's the first thing I asked Fritz. He said the bruising looked more like a pinch. Like someone was grabbing him instead of slamming him."

"A pinch? Weird." I thought about it as I chewed another bite. "Maybe someone was grabbing him." I reached out and plucked at the air. "Maybe they saw him falling and reached out, and the only thing they could grab was his chest."

"Sort of far-fetched. His arms would have been flailing. They would have been the first place to grab. And that theory doesn't go with what the witnesses heard. If someone was trying to keep you from falling head first down the stairs, you wouldn't yell at them to go away."

"Good point. And good burgers too. Thanks. I didn't realize how hungry I was until the first bite." I picked up a fry and briefly considered that I might be eating too fast. Lana loved to point out when I was acting like a human vacuum. I made a mental note to ignore my hunger and eat more like a lady than a vacuum. "Anything else new on the case?"

"It's a frustrating one. If the two witnesses hadn't heard Kenneth pleading with someone before the fall, this would have been written off as an accident. But I have to treat it like a possible murder. And to answer your question more directly—the yellow strand I showed you in the evidence bag seems to have come from a synthetic wig."

"A wig?" I thought back to all the people in Dandelion Inn that night. "No one was wearing a wig. In fact it's not all that common these days."

"I called Kitty Bloomfield to ask if she had anyone through the inn lately who wore a wig. She said a group of older women, who were in town for a quilting bee, had stayed at the inn last week. She was certain she remembered two of them wearing wigs."

"Huh, I take back my generalization then. That might explain the strand of synthetic hair."

Jackson put down his burger. "Except, as you noted already, Kitty is obsessed with cleanliness. She was very insulted when I suggested the strand of hair could have sat there for more than a week. I didn't push the point because I didn't want to get the housekeeper in trouble."

"She does keep a spectacularly clean inn. It's kind of daunting to think about keeping this place that clean when I finally open to guests."

A raspberry-ish sound fluttered behind me. I froze mid-bite. I hadn't sensed Edward's presence but then that might have been because of the enormous presence Jackson cast as he sat in my kitchen.

Jackson's brow furrowed as if he'd heard the sound. But that was impossible. I was relieved when he moved on from it. "During our conversation, Kitty mentioned that Barbara had been released after her antacid overdose." We exchanged amused smiles. "They are all getting restless. She said Jamie and Rex rented a car. They've decided to take a road trip and look at a few more haunted destinations. I don't see how I can keep them here any longer. And you'll be interested to know that I did some digging, after you mentioned the call from the lawyer on Angela's phone. It turns out Kenneth Applegate inherited all of his dad's money. Angela had a different mother and the divorce was so bitter, Martin Applegate took it out on the ex-wife by taking her and Angela out of the will."

"How cruel. That means Kenneth had all the family money."

Jackson dipped a fry into ketchup. "Not anymore. Kenneth had no other immediate family except Angela. According to the lawyer, she'll be getting everything."

"Ah ha, a possible motive."

"Might be," he said.

I moved onto a new subject that had less to do with murder and motives. One that hopefully wouldn't warrant ungentlemanly noises from my ghost. "You call me Bluebird and occasionally my real name, but I don't have a friendly moniker for you. Not for when we are working in our professional capacities, of course, but, like now, when we're just hanging out eating burgers. Detective Jackson seems kind of formal."

"Sir Brady Jackson," he suggested with a crooked grin.

"Everyone calls me Jax. I don't really like the name Brady. People always inevitably break into the Brady Bunch theme song when someone calls me by my name."

I chuckled. "I'd never put those two things together, but now that you've made the connection for me—"

"Oh great," he said.

"I'll just call you Jax. I like it."

His amber eyes looked nearly dark gold under the kitchen light. He gazed at me in a different way than usual. "And I like the way it sounds coming from your lips."

My entire body tightened with adrenaline at his comment. I hadn't dated since my horrid breakup with Brett, but I was certain I still recognized flirting when I heard it. He leaned toward me. Suddenly, I was sure he would kiss me. I had trouble balancing on the stool as he moved his face closer to mine. I closed my eyes as he neared. I held my breath in anticipation.

Thunk, clink, bang! Newman's tennis ball shot past us, bounced off the oven and hit the pots and pans hanging over the table. Jackson stood up abruptly and looked around the otherwise empty kitchen. Thankfully, Newman had jumped up excitedly when he heard the ball. He was the only excuse I could muster. After the near kiss followed by Edward's tantrum, I was having a hard time sorting my thoughts.

"That dog of mine," I laughed and the fakeness was grating on my ears. "He's somehow figured out how to toss a ball with his mouth. That's how desperate he is to have the ball thrown."

Jackson stared down at me with disbelief. "That was not a toss from a dog's muzzle. That thing fired across the room like a bullet." He reached up and touched the side of his face. "Nearly took my ear off."

"Well, look around. There's no one else here except the dogs." The waver in my tone wasn't helping prove my point.

Jackson glanced around the room once more before sitting

down with a good deal of hesitation. "Fine, but I'm going to be watching that dog to see how he does it. Or maybe this place is more haunted than you think," he added as his phone rang in his pocket.

He pulled it out to see who was calling. "Speaking of haunted inns, it's Kitty Bloomfield." He stood up. "Excuse me." He walked out of the room to take the call.

Edward immediately appeared on his perch over the hearth. "You were going to let him kiss you."

I moved closer to the hearth, so I could talk quietly. "Yes, yes I was. Until you interfered," I hissed.

Edward, on the other hand, spoke as loudly and freely as he pleased. "Someone had to. It's obvious you're a bad decision maker. He should not be here without a chaperone."

"Chaperones only exist at school dances," I whispered sharply.

That started a new discussion. "They allow dancing in schools? No wonder the human race is faltering so badly in everything proper and moral."

I blinked up at him, flabbergasted and frankly not sure what to do with him.

"As I've said before—" Edward continued . . . unfortunately. "I don't like him." He vanished as Jackson's heavy footsteps sounded in the hallway.

Jackson reached the kitchen and looked around with a profoundly confused expression.

"Everything all right?" I asked.

He glanced over at the dogs who had dropped down on their pillows. "Either those two dogs can talk or I'm losing my mind. I could have sworn I heard a male voice when I was heading back to the kitchen. Here's something even crazier. I could have sworn he had a British accent."

I froze in shock, not sure what to say or do or think. Maybe Edward was losing his ghostly skills. He always made sure only I could see or hear him. Unless he wanted someone else to hear. That was it. He wanted Jackson to know he didn't approve. He was trying to scare him off. My shock turned to anger. I had to unclench my jaw to speak.

"I haven't heard my dogs talk but then you never know. They *are* border collies." I laughed airily or as airily as I could. "I think you've just been working too long of hours, Detective Jackson."

He raked back his thick hair with his fingers. "You might be right. Which brings me to the next subject. There's trouble at Dandelion Inn. Kitty was too upset to articulate what was going on. I just hope it's not another antacid overdose. I've got to cut short the burger date."

"That's a shame." A thought popped into my head.

He seemed to read my mind. "You want to go along, don't you?"

I pressed my finger coyly to my lips. (The lips that were almost kissed tonight.) "Could I?"

"Maybe it's not such a bad idea. You seem to be pretty good at calming Kitty down."

"Yippee. I'm going on a ride-along with the Firefly Junction police."

CHAPTER 28

*J*ackson told me about his childhood and his two big brothers, who teased him mercilessly. He didn't bring up the disembodied voice in my house, and I was just as glad not to think about it. By the time we arrived at Dandelion Inn, the rain had fizzled to a mist, but the moisture evaporating off the road produced an eerie haze.

Jackson parked the car. "That fog makes the Dandelion Inn look like it belongs on the set of a scary movie."

"I was just thinking the same thing." There was no one on the porch or outside the house but then it was dark and wet. "I don't see people running from the house or an ambulance so maybe that's a good sign," I said.

"Kitty muttered something about a portrait and violent damage. Or at least I think that was what she said. She was hyperventilating and taking such sharp breaths in between it was hard to understand."

We climbed out of the car. I pulled my coat closer. "Seems like winter is trying to push its way into autumn."

"These look slippery." Jackson placed a protective hand against my back as we climbed the wet steps to the porch. Even through cool mist and my raincoat, I could still feel the heat of his hand seconds after he dropped it.

Lucy, the chef, opened the door. "Detective Jackson," she said breathlessly. "This way. We fixed Kitty some tea. It helped calm her down, but we're all so distraught."

"Is someone hurt?" Jackson asked as we followed Lucy past the stairs. The cleaning crew had done a stellar job. There was no sign of the terrible fatal fall.

"No one is hurt, but there's been some violence," Lucy said over her shoulder. She was wearing a blue robe over pajamas. "I just don't know who would do such a thing."

Lucy ushered us into the dining room. Kitty was sitting, shoulders hunched and swollen eyes, at a table. Angela had a comforting hand on Kitty's arm. Barbara sat at the same table looking shaken. Her hand trembled as she brought her tea cup to her mouth. Everyone except Rex was dressed for bed.

Rex and Wilma were standing across the room staring up at the portrait of Lauren Grace. There was no sign of Jamie Nielsen.

"There you are, Jackson," Rex's voice boomed in the quiet room. "What do you think of this? Strangest case of vandalism I've ever seen. Makes no sense."

Jackson and I walked over to the fireplace where the ornately framed portrait of Lauren Grace hung.

I covered my mouth to stifle a gasp. The canvas, Miss Grace's beautiful face included, had been shredded as if a tiger had run its sharp claws down the painting several times. It was unsalvageable.

Jackson was the only person tall enough to get a close look at the damage. He put his face right up to the torn painting. "Looks like a knife or possibly a razor."

"I was wrong then," Wilma said meekly. She held up a letter opener. "I found this squeezed between those two chafing dishes on the buffet. I know it wasn't there the last time I dusted the buffet, and I've never seen Kitty open mail in the dining room. The letter opener is usually on the desk in the kitchen."

Jackson's mouth twisted in frustration. "Could you just lay it on the mantel. Try not to touch any more than the handle section between your fingers. I need to collect it for evidence. I'd say your theory is a good one."

Wilma couldn't hold back a smile. "I'll just place it here gently. I promise I didn't touch it too much."

Jackson and I walked over and sat at the table with the women. The first time I met Kitty she was a bright-eyed, energetic woman with a pretty pile of pinkish-blonde curls. It was hard to believe that was only two days ago. She was a thin, frail shell of her former self. This had undoubtedly made the list for worst weeks at Dandelion Inn.

Jackson reached over and touched Kitty's hand. "I know this has been a stressful week, Miss Bloomfield, but can you tell me what happened?"

Her thin shoulders jolted up and down. "I wish I knew. Everyone was tired and weary from—well, you know. So I had Lucy cook up a nice split pea soup and some of her cornbread. With the rainy weather and all, it was just what everyone needed. We finished the whole pot," she said with a slightly happier tone. "Everyone decided to go to bed since they were going to be traveling back home tomorrow. Lucy, Wilma and I were exhausted from the terrible week."

"Is Jamie Nielsen still in bed?" Jackson asked.

Kitty looked around and seemed to realize for the first time that one of the guests was missing.

"Jamie left right after dinner," Rex interjected. "Said he had some errands to do before we take off on our road trip."

"And the painting was untouched at dinner?" Jackson asked.

Kitty nearly scoffed. "Of course. We would have noticed it

otherwise. In fact, every night, before I go to bed, I make a point of tapping the mantel right under the painting. Then I say, "Good night, Lauren. No mischief please."

Lucy nodded. "She does. *Every* night." There was a twinge of sarcasm behind her words.

"I can tell you Lauren Grace was as lovely as ever when I said good night to her after dinner," Kitty said.

"What happened next?" Jackson asked.

"The usual. Everyone got ready for bed and lights went out. The house was silent and peaceful for the first time in two days." Kitty took a deep, shuddering breath. "Then Wilma started yelling. I was hoping it was just a dream because I didn't need another tragedy."

Jackson turned to Wilma, who shifted in her seat and straightened her posture, suddenly aware all eyes were on her.

"I came back downstairs for a drink of water. I get thirsty at night, and I don't care for the tap water in the bathroom. It tastes funny." She crinkled her nose cutely, which I felt strongly was a gesture just for Jackson. "Anyhow, I came down here and walked straight into the kitchen for the water. Naturally, I had no reason to look back at the portrait. I dust that gold frame every day. I see Miss Grace plenty. But when I walked back out, the lights from the kitchen appliances lit the dining room up for a second. My eyes just happened to drift toward the painting. The room went dark when the kitchen door shut, but I knew something didn't look right. Miss Grace's white dress had stripes. I hurried over to switch on the light and just about fainted. That's when I started yelling for Kitty. She came downstairs a few minutes later."

Jackson looked at Angela. "And you, Miss Applegate? Did you hear or see anything?"

Angela had dark rings under her eyes. "I took some cold medicine. I don't have a cold, but it helps me sleep. Kenny's death has given me insomnia," she added. "I was just dropping into a deep sleep when I heard agitated voices in the hallway. It took me a few minutes to shake the grogginess from my head. I grabbed my robe and went downstairs to see what was happening."

Lucy gave close to the same account, sans the cold medicine and insomnia issue. Barbara was extremely quiet while everyone else spoke. She'd had an ordeal herself and had only recently been released from the hospital. She was taking Kenneth's death very hard. She'd been happy and exuberant when she was at Cider Ridge, but she looked like a fragile, shy child at the moment.

"Miss Simpson." Jackson saying her name seemed to pop Barbara out of a trance.

"Yes?" she asked as if she hadn't just heard Jackson ask everyone seated at the table the same question.

"I wonder if you could tell me if you saw or heard anything."

Barbara tightened the belt on her robe. "I was sleeping. I sleep like a rock. Slept right through an apartment fire when I was a child. Woke up outside on the front lot in my mom's arms and had no idea anything had happened. But I did hear people downstairs. I put on my robe and went down thinking possibly there had been a sighting."

"A sighting?" Jackson asked.

"Of Lauren Grace, of course," Barbara said plainly.

"Oh, right." Jackson stood up. "I'm going to go out to the car and get a few things. I need to bag up the letter opener for evidence."

"The letter opener?" Kitty asked in surprise.

"I found your letter opener right over there between the two silver chafing dishes," Wilma piped up. "Did you leave it there?"

Kitty placed her hand on her chest. "Never. I always leave it on Lucy's desk in the kitchen."

Wilma grinned and nodded at Jackson. "See, I told you so."

"Yes, yes you did." He stopped before leaving the room. "Has anyone seen or talked to Mr. Nielsen since dinner?"

Rex nodded. "Just a quick conversation. I was smoking a cigar on the porch. I asked him where he was going. He told me he had errands to run. Seemed kind of late for it but that's what he said. Haven't seen him since."

I couldn't get a clear sense of what Jackson was thinking but it seemed he had some suspicions about Jamie Nielsen.

CHAPTER 29

*J*ackson got a call the second he pulled up to my house. He glanced at his phone. "It's the station."

"You poor man, no one leaves you alone. Don't worry about walking me to the house. I can find my way. Go ahead and take the call. Thanks for the burger and the adventure."

I was almost relieved not to have him walk me to the door. The entire kiss moment had been ruined by Edward, I was sure it just wasn't meant to be tonight. A shadow on the porch startled me, until Redford's eyes caught the moonlight above.

"Why on earth are you outside?" I reached the porch and discovered Newman was outside as well. Both looked sheepish and sad as if they'd been up to something or something had frightened them. What was Edward up to now?

Jackson's car still idled out in front of the house. I heard him drive slowly away as I unlocked the door and went inside. The dogs entered but then sat firmly in the entryway, determined not to go any farther.

"Edward," I called. "What are you up to? Why are the dogs outside?"

Edward appeared directly in front of me. I stumbled back a step. "There you are. What have you done to the dogs?"

Edward stared at me with a perplexed expression. "You were out?"

"Yes. I just got back and found my dogs outside on the porch."

He glanced at the dogs. "They *are* animals, after all, but I assure you I didn't send them out there. But I'm still confused."

"About what?"

"If you just got in, then who is shuffling around your bedroom?"

His question sent a streak of cold fear through me, but I quickly rationalized it. "No wonder the dogs were on the porch, looking like frightened rabbits," I said pointedly to both of them. Ears went down in response. "It must be those blasted raccoons again. They come in through the dog door, and I forgot to shut it before I left."

I hurried down the hallway and grabbed a spoon and pot from the kitchen to make a clatter. I heard the slightest sound coming from my bedroom as if the raccoons knew they'd been caught and were freezing in place.

I banged the pot and threw open my bedroom door. A body that was absolutely not a raccoon slammed into me so hard it knocked me back against the hallway wall. I fell hard on my bottom. I caught a glimpse of Jamie Nielsen's eyes as he raced past. He was holding the envelope with the pictures from Lola's Antiques.

I pushed to my feet and raced after him. For no apparent reason, the lights started flickering on and off in the house. A thud and a grunt followed and I nearly pitched headlong over Jamie, who was splayed face first in the hallway.

"You can't have those pictures."

Jamie pushed to his feet, the envelope clutched tightly in his hand. "Ah ha, so they are real. You have a ghost in the house. He's standing right on the porch." He lifted the envelope. "These pictures will make my career. No more hanging out in stupid meaningless societies like Applegate's. He was an actor, not a true talent."

"Oh, so you're a true talent," I said wryly as I winked at the ghost hovering literally inches from him.

"Darn right. And with these pictures, I will be at the top of the profession."

I couldn't let him take them. I lunged for the envelope. He swung his arm in defense. It was big and hard enough to push me back several steps. I leaned over to catch the wind he had knocked from me. My ribs ached from the impact.

A clamor in the entryway helped me regain my composure. Footsteps pounded the floor. "Sunni!" Jackson's deep voice echoed through the house. Nielsen blanched at the sound of it.

"In here," I called.

Jackson deconstructed the scene quickly and immediately understood that Nielsen had not been an invited guest. His face grew tight with anger as he spun Nielsen around, grabbed the front of his shirt and pressed him against the hallway wall. The envelope fluttered to the ground, and I quickly retrieved it. "There better be a good reason that she is holding her stomach, and it better not have anything to do with you."

Nielsen sealed his mouth in fear.

"I came in and found him rummaging through my room for this envelope." My words trembled.

"In that case"—Jackson yanked Jamie's arm around and behind his back—"You are under arrest for breaking and entering—"

"The back door was unlocked," Nielsen complained.

Jackson put his mouth closer to Nielsen's ear. "Were you invited in through that unlocked door?"

"No."

"Then I'm arresting you for breaking and entering and every other thing I can pin on you. I'll be thinking about the list as I walk you out to the car." Jackson didn't look back as he took Nielsen out the door.

I needed to sit down. I shuffled to the kitchen and climbed weakly up on a stool. I winced at the pain in my ribs and my tailbone.

"Should I get you something?" Edward asked as he materialized across the table.

"No, it's still just the shock."

I glanced toward the hallway at the sound of claws clicking on wood floors. Both dogs came to sit by me with apologetic smiles. I pet each one on the head. "A tad more bravery might be nice. After all, I named you after two cool Hollywood bad boys."

"They are just a step above having a cat when it comes to security." Edward looked pointedly at the envelope I'd placed on the table. "I hope it was worth it."

Red lights flashed in the kitchen window signaling that Jackson had called a squad car to come pick Nielsen up.

We were alone. I pulled out the pictures and passed them across the table. Edward's long white fingers picked them up. "It's Mary, Mary Richards," he said and passed the pictures back to me. "She lived here long ago with three very annoying children. But I liked Mary. She was one of the few people—"

"That you communicated with?" I asked. "Like me?"

"Yes. She was witty too but not nearly as smart." The voices outside drew him to the window. "Perhaps I was too quick to judge him," he said still looking out the window.

"Takes a big man to admit when he's wrong."

He swung back around. "I didn't say I was wrong. I said quick to judge. I still had to call him back with my light trick."

"So you're the reason the lights were going on and off. Thought light flickering was beneath you."

"This was different. I wasn't trying to scare someone. I thought it would catch his attention before his vehicle was out of view. Seems my plan worked," he said proudly.

"It did." I got up from the stool to get a drink of water. "Did you make sure he heard you earlier this evening? When we were talking in the kitchen, it seemed he heard your voice. Even mentioned the accent."

"I don't have an accent. *You* people have the accents. And no, he should not have heard me."

"Yet, he did."

Edward vanished at the sound of footsteps in the hallway. Jackson was wearing the cutest amount of concern in his face.

"Sunni, are you all right?" He walked straight to me and took hold of my hand. The gesture made my heart flutter.

"Yes, I'm fine, thanks to you." I peered up at him, but it took some courage with his closeness and those amazing amber eyes. "You came back."

"That was because of your clever trick with the lights."

"Y—yes," I stuttered, "wasn't that clever of me. I'm just glad you got here."

"What is in that envelope that made Nielsen commit a crime to get to it?"

Not sure how to answer and feeling too out of sorts to come up with anything plausible, I deftly ignored his question by tossing out one of my own. "Do you think Nielsen did it? Is he the one who pushed Kenneth down the stairs?"

"They are two unrelated crimes, but if he's capable of breaking into a home and pushing a woman around, then he could just be capable of murder. But it might help if I know what's in the envelope."

So much for my deftness. "It's just some research about Cider

Ridge Inn. I'm gathering information to write up a story about its sordid history. Nielsen was staying here when the envelope arrived and unbeknownst to me, he was reading it over my shoulder. I guess he thought it was information that would bolster the rumor that the house was haunted." I decided it wasn't really a lie. I'd just left out the detail that they were conclusive photos of a ghost. "While we were in the midst of our struggle, he told me he was going to become the head of the paranormal community. He added in a few insults about Kenneth at the same time. I thought that might be significant. He thought poorly of Kenneth's abilities."

"At the moment, the only thing he's going to need is a lawyer. They're taking him in right now, and since I have him in custody, I'm going to press him about Kenneth's fall."

My stomach sank to my knees. Surely Jamie was going to tell Jackson about the photos. And who was I kidding? I lied to the man about the contents of the envelope. I hated the thought of Jackson thinking of me as a liar.

"Um, do I have to press charges for him to be arrested?"

Jackson squinted down at me, trying to figure out where I was going with this. "Yes."

"It's just I don't think he meant to hurt me. I was fighting to get the envelope back, and he pushed me away. And I *did* leave the back door unlocked."

Edward materialized behind Jackson with a fierce glower.

"What are you saying, Sunni? You don't want me to arrest him?"

I shrugged. "I don't think he'll come back." I shivered slightly at the thought of him wandering through my bedroom. "He's leaving tomorrow with Rex on a road trip. I don't think he meant harm. He's just obsessed with ghosts. Besides, how can a man who wears Birkenstock sandals be dangerous?" My attempt at humor fell flat.

Jackson was not happy. "Fine, I'll tell them to let him go," he said curtly and turned to leave.

"Don't be mad, Jackson. I still appreciate you coming back

here," I said weakly, knowing that anger had already turned off his *listening* ears.

He walked out the door and down the steps to the police car without another word. One minute I was close to being kissed, the next I was on the receiving end of a sharp heel turn. What a rotten way to end the evening.

I turned and headed back to the kitchen. Edward was perched on the hearth with his arms crossed. He was just about to add his unnecessary lecture to the mix. I wasn't in the mood.

"Not a word, Edward. Not a word." I plucked the envelope from the table, walked into my bedroom and shut the door sharply.

CHAPTER 30

Occasionally, I needed my friend Raine more than I needed my sisters. Today was one of those days. Naturally, both of my sisters had texted me the second I walked into my bedroom. They could both see the flashing red lights in front of my house and were worried. I assured them everything was fine but didn't have the spirit or enthusiasm to replay the night for them. As the older sister, Lana was much better at handing out opinions than listening. She would surely lecture me about the wrong decision I'd made in not charging Nielsen. And Emily lived such a heavenly, charmed existence with her doting, wonderful husband and her animals . . . and then there were Cuddlebug and Tinkerbell. No one could have a bad day if they had little goats prancing around the yard. I'd texted Raine almost the second I sat down at my desk to make sure she was available for lunch. I needed to rant and whine and chastise myself to a good listener. And Raine was a good listener. A skill she'd probably honed during her years of trying to communicate with spirits. And that was the second reason for our lunch date. I needed to find out what she knew about the ghost at Dandelion Inn. Edward certainly existed and could do things like scare intruders or slam shut doors. It seemed plausible that Kenneth had met up with Lauren Grace's spirit. Only instead of Rex's theory that Lauren got tired of Kenneth's obsession with her, I'd come up with a possible scenario of my own. If Kenneth was truly just a fake like Nielsen purported, then his reaction coming face to face with an actual ghost might have scared him into the fall. I had no proof of any of it, but I was desperately looking for an angle for my article and Raine was my go-to source on the spirit world.

I'd hoped to get out of the office before Parker arrived. He was going to be late, and Myrna wasn't sure if he'd be in at all. He was certain he'd developed an allergy to his wife's cat and was heading to an allergist to find out for sure.

Parker barreled into the newspaper office ten minutes before my lunch break. He was a large, brusque man for having such a delicate constitution. "Taylor," he barked. "What are you working on now that the Applegate thing fell apart?" He laughed. "Or, I guess I should say fell down. What's your angle going to be, and it better be good. That labor dispute piece Chase sent me is as dry and dull as reading the cereal box."

"I'm working on the new angle. It has to do with the accident and the vandalism of the portrait." I realized as soon as I said it that he wouldn't have heard anything about the painting yet. "Last night there was an incident at Dandelion Inn. The famous portrait of the original owner and apparent ghost at the inn was slashed. Damaged beyond repair. I'm going to head back there after lunch to do some snooping around." I hadn't planned to revisit the Dandelion today, but the idea popped into my head. I figured it would convince my editor into thinking I was hot on the trail of something noteworthy.

"That's good. Follow that story. The town council is already upset that our chances of hosting the paranormal convention have just been quashed by Applegate's death. Maybe all is not lost yet. If there is something strange going on at that inn, I'm sure you'll uncover it." He was putting a heaping serving of trust on me, which only served to break my confidence.

Parker walked into his office and shut the door.

Myrna looked across the room at me. "It's not fair that he puts all the pressure on you to write something dazzling for the paper. He doesn't even bother to expect anything from Chase, his lead reporter."

I pulled on my coat. "I don't mind the pressure. I just hope I can deliver. I'm going to head over to Dandelion Inn after lunch. With any luck, a ghost will jump out of a closet and take a few selfies with me. That oughta sell some papers. See you later, Myrna."

"Good luck with the ghost selfies."

I walked to Layers. I pulled my coat closer to shield myself from the cool breeze drizzling through the trees. Fall was definitely in the air. Rain from the night before had left a distinctive almost smoky fragrance wafting off of the asphalt and sidewalk. The downpour had lasted a short time but had been hostile enough to wash piles of dead leaves and debris into the road. If it had lasted another hour, it would have washed the same residue away.

Raine was wearing a bright yellow knit beanie as she approached Layers from the opposite side where her psychic shop was located. Her bangles glittered as she waved at me.

"Ballard added some new sandwiches to the menu. She does it every fall when the weather starts to cool. Get this," she said enthusiastically. "The Marlon Brando is a deconstructed roast beef sandwich in a bread bowl that's filled with mashed potatoes, carrots, roast beef and gravy."

"That sounds delicious," I said. "But since I'm not running a twenty-six mile marathon this afternoon, I might opt for something lighter." I rubbed my stomach. It was still a little sore. "Besides, I crave a good long chat more than food today."

She put her arm around me. "Well then, you've asked the right person to lunch. Let's go inside and you can tell me all about your exciting evening with detectives and police cars and flashing lights."

"I guess my sister already filled you in on my night."

"Yes but she was seriously lacking details."

The aroma of roast beef struck us as we walked inside. Apparently the cold weather had made Marlon Brando the popular choice for the day. If I'd had a better appetite, I would have ordered one.

We walked to a table near the back and sat down.

Raine's yellow beanie was so bright it almost hurt my eyes. She seemed to sense it and pulled it off. "So, my friend, let's hear the whole story and don't leave out any of the good stuff."

CHAPTER 31

*R*aine drifted into an intoxicated state with her luscious
bread bowl brimming with mashed potatoes, roast and
gravy while I picked at my Debbie Reynolds, hummus, cucumber
and avocado on whole wheat toast. My appetite was still dimmed
by the chaotic night.

"I still can't believe there was a near kiss," Raine said just before
a bite of potato.

"I guess it's silly to dwell on it because it never happened, so I
can't really categorize it as a near kiss. It was just a leaning toward
the possibility of a kiss."

"Yes but it was the possibility of a kiss from Detective Jackson.
Not just some average Joe from down the road." She sat back with
a proud smile. "My best friend was nearly kissed by Detective
Brady Jackson. I'm jealous and proud all at once." She followed her
shallow boast with a sigh.

After telling Raine all the details of the crazy night, intruder
included, she was still focused on the near kiss. I regretted even
mentioning it. I was starting to feel like a school girl just talking

about it. I picked up my sandwich but put it down when a text came through. There I was being a school girl again, hoping the text was from the boy who almost kissed me. It was from Lana.

"I heard the painting of Lauren Grace was destroyed," Lana texted.

"Yep, I'm at lunch with Raine. I'll tell you about it later."

Raine waited with anticipation. "So was it him? Was it Jackson?"

"Sorry to burst your bubble but it was Lana." I wiped my hands on my napkin, deciding I'd had enough Debbie Reynolds. "You don't seem that surprised about what Jamie Nielsen did."

Raine shrugged. "Like I said, I don't know him that well except that he's somewhat delusional about his talents. What did you say he was after? An envelope with research inside of it?"

I'd had no choice except to tell Raine the same lie I'd told Jackson. If there was ever a time when I wanted to tell everything, just spill the entire secret to my best friend, it was today. But it wasn't my secret to tell. It was Edward's.

"Yes, it's all about the history of Cider Ridge. Jamie was snooping over my shoulder as I was scanning the—the information. Must have been something in there he thought was important." I was counting on the fact that Jamie had left town with Rex this morning, never to return. Otherwise, I was going to have some cleaning up to do.

"I don't quite understand what he could have possibly gleamed from the inn's history but then Jamie likes to write books about haunted places. Maybe he thought Cider Ridge would make a good subject. I can tell you there are more vibrations and disturbances in your house than in any other place I've been." She leaned forward and lowered her voice. "I could swear sometimes we are being watched when we are sitting in your kitchen having lunch or coffee. He's there, I'm sure of it."

I smiled stiffly. "You might be right."

"I know I'm right." She returned to her Marlon Brando. "This is delicious but I'm going to need a nap after lunch. Good thing I don't have anything on my calendar. And Lana is still working on purchase orders for the wedding receptions. I might just take a hot bath and kick my feet up for the rest of the day."

"Or," I said excitedly, "you could go with me to Dandelion Inn. I've asked Kitty for permission to snoop around a bit and look for evidence in the destruction of the portrait. Poor thing is so exhausted from the week, she basically sighed in surrender at my request. She told me 'you might as well. The week is a lost cause anyhow'. She really is a sweet lady."

Raine lifted up both her palms like trays on an old fashioned scale. She lifted her right palm. "Hmm, let me see, hot bath and nap." She lifted her left palm. "Or snooping around an old inn that I already know doesn't have much happening other than the usual creaks and moans of an old house." She held them even for a second, and it looked like bath and nap were going to win. "What the heck, I'll go."

"Perfect. Wait did you say you knew about the hauntings at Dandelion Inn?"

"Hauntings? I'd hardly call them that. I was invited by a group of women who were on a girls' weekend at the inn. They asked me to do a séance and summon Lauren Grace. I performed it, of course. *Some* people like my séance's." She looked pointedly at me. "Only I knew almost the moment I sat down at the table that there was nothing in the house that could be conjured, summoned, or communicated with. I've heard tales of Lauren Grace's ghost in that house, but I've never felt her presence."

"Interesting. Although, I will admit, the few recollections of supposed encounters with Lauren Grace were underwhelming at best. Still, something strange is going on in that house. When Kenneth fell, he pleaded with someone to leave him alone and go away. Then the painting gets destroyed while everyone is upstairs in bed. Of course, Nielsen wasn't. He was busy staking out my house, apparently waiting for me to leave so he could break in."

"That does make him look suspicious, don't you think?" Raine asked. "I mean if he was capable of entering someone's home uninvited—"

"Then he's capable of murder?" I asked skeptically.

Raine pursed her lips. "Yeah, I guess one doesn't necessarily follow the other. Do you think Kitty will mind if I tag along?"

"Not if we tell her you are there to try and communicate with Lauren. After all, if she is lingering in the house, there'd be no better witness to both crimes. In fact, Rex Thunder thinks Lauren got sick of Kenneth ogling her portrait and scared him right off the top steps to his death. I confess, I've wondered the same thing."

"That seems far-fetched. Maybe Rex came up with that theory to cover for his own misdeed."

I pulled out my wallet. "I'll pay for lunch since you're doing me this favor."

"Woo hoo, that made this Marlon Brando even more delicious."

I took out the money and placed it under the check. "I know Jackson thought the same thing when Rex announced his theory. Then there's the matter of money—always a good motive for murder."

We got up from the table and waved to Ballard on our way out. Clouds had moved in, making the day, all at once, colder and gloomier.

Raine pulled her yellow beanie down on her head. I couldn't hold back a laugh. "That cap takes yellow to a whole other level."

"It's lemon yellow," Raine said with a chin lift.

"No, it's atomic yellow. People flying overhead in jetliners can track your movements along the sidewalk."

"Funny." She straightened the beanie. "I like it. Anyhow, what money motive are you talking about?"

"It seems Kenneth Applegate's father was a bit of a bohemian ghost chaser. Traveled around the country in the sixties in a Volkswagen bus. In reality, he was heir to a large fortune."

"Yes, Martin Applegate is still a big name in paranormal circles. He was far more naturally talented than his son. Or at least that is what I've heard. And I knew he was wealthy. I think the family was in real estate."

We reached my jeep. "For someone who claims to be independent from the *paranormal circles*, you sure know a lot about them."

"Just because I don't traipse around the country with them doesn't mean I shouldn't be informed."

"True." We climbed into the jeep and I turned it on to the get the heat started.

Raine watched me fiddle with the controls. "Guess it's official. Air conditioner season is gone and it's time to crank the heat."

"I personally love the change of seasons." I pulled out to the road.

"Me too. It lets me pull out all my brightly colored beanies," she said with a satisfied grin. "Who would get rich if Kenneth died?"

"His sister, Angela. Or I should say, half sister. They had different moms. Martin had a falling out with Angela's mother, so he cut them out of the will. Kenneth had no other family so the bulk of his money will go to Angela."

"Interesting. Is Angela a suspect?"

"She has motive but there just isn't much evidence to charge anyone. Jax doesn't admit it, but I think he's in a muddle. The only thing he has to go on is the two witnesses claiming they heard Kenneth pleading on the stairs." I could feel Raine staring at the side of my face as I watched the road. "What?" I asked.

"So it's Jax now, eh?"

"That's what you picked up on?" I wriggled in the seat and straightened my posture. "And yes, that's what he told me to call him. I like it."

"No argument from me. I just thought it was interesting that you were on a nickname basis already."

"For your information, he's had a nickname for me since he first met me at the Alder Stevens murder scene." I regretted the statement the second I said it.

Raine twisted sideways on the seat. "Is that right? And what might that nickname be?"

"You sound just like Lana when you're being annoying."

"Thank you, I consider that a compliment. Out with it. What does the dreamiest detective this side of the Mississippi call you?"

I stared straight ahead at the road. "You're the psychic. Figure it out yourself."

She sat back against the seat. "I'll do just that."

CHAPTER 32

*I*t seemed as if our conversation about Detective Jackson had made him think of me. My phone rang just as I parked in front of Dandelion Inn. Raine knew exactly who it was when I looked up from my phone screen.

"Fine, I'll wait outside." She reluctantly climbed out of the car.

"Hey, Sunni, sorry I didn't call earlier. I've been at the court-house all morning. I just wanted to check in and see how you were feeling." There was a note of disappointment in Jackson's voice. He was still upset with my decision not to press charges against Jamie.

"I'm fine, thanks. Jax, I'm sorry about last night. I know you wanted to take Nielsen into the station but—I just didn't want to get tied up in something like that. Besides, I think his motives were purely to advance his standing in the paranormal world. There was no malicious intent."

"Except that he pushed you."

"Yes, he was wrong to be so defensive. I just hope you can understand."

"Might take time. I wanted to let you know we got several

fingerprints off the letter opener. I just need to get fingerprints from everyone in the house. I know Barbara and Angela are still at the inn for another day, recuperating before their trip home. Unfortunately, I won't be able to get the other prints. I called Kitty this morning, hoping to get prints before the men left. It seems they were anxious to get out of town. They left before dawn. I guess neither man was too broken up by Kenneth's death."

"Sorry again. I guess you would have already had Jamie's prints if things had gone differently last night."

"Can't focus on that now. I don't even know if the two crimes are related. I've got a bunch of other stuff on my plate. If I don't find anything else that marks this as murder, I may close it as an accident."

"There's nothing else to do?" I asked.

"I might interview everyone who was inside the house that night once more to see if there are any inconsistencies, but since his death was caused by the fall, it's much harder to pin a murder charge on someone. These kinds of cases, fatal falls and the like, are always tricky."

Raine was standing outside the Dandelion in her yellow beanie, crossing her arms to ward off the chill in the air.

"I've just arrived at Dandelion Inn," I said. "Kitty said it would be all right if I had another look around. I'm struggling to write my article, and I'm hoping for some inspiration."

"Good luck with that. Let me know if you find something significant."

"You'll be the first person I call," I said cheerily. But the tone coming from the other side of the phone was stilted. I hated to hear it.

"Talk to you later," Jackson said and hung up.

I climbed out of the jeep. Raine waved her hand to hurry me along.

"I need to drag out my winter coats," Raine said as I reached the front steps.

It took a few minutes for the front door to open. It was Wilma. Her hair was tied back in a red bandana and she was holding a feather duster. "Hello, Kitty mentioned you were coming. She's in the dining room polishing silver." Wilma shut the front door behind us as we stepped into the entry. "She claims polishing silver helps with her nerves," Wilma said quietly. "I'm just glad she likes to do it. I've got enough to do to keep this place spotless." She waved the duster. Kitty's house was so clean, no dust fell from the feathers.

Wilma led us through to the dining room. Raine leaned her head toward mine. "Is that the infamous staircase?" she whispered.

"Yes," I whispered back.

Kitty's thin arm was twittering back and forth as she rubbed polish into a silver serving dish.

"Kitty, you have visitors."

Kitty didn't hear her so Wilma repeated it. She looked up for the first time and gave her arm a rest.

"Wow, talk about elbow grease," I quipped as I looked over the collection of silver platters and serving dishes. "Such a beautiful collection of silver."

The compliment worked its charm. The stern expression Kitty was wearing when we walked into the room melted into a sweet grin. "Thank you. They belonged to my mother."

Kitty smiled up at Raine. "Now don't tell me. I pride myself at being a whiz with names. It's something to do with the weather." She pointed. "Raine, right? I remember when you came to perform the séance. I'm afraid Lauren wasn't being very cooperative that night." Then Kitty's face saddened. Her mention of Lauren had reminded her of the ruined portrait. It was no longer hanging over the mantel.

"It's good to see you again, Ms. Bloomfield," Raine said.

It wasn't my place to tell Kitty about the fingerprints on the letter opener and I didn't need to do anything else to upset Jackson, so I left it out of the conversation. "If you don't mind," I said, "I'd like to take a walk around with Raine. It seems to me if anyone knows what happened to your lovely painting, it would be Lauren Grace, herself. That's where Raine comes in handy. I've witnessed her extra sensory perception on many occasions." I could sense Raine's posture straightening with pride as I spoke. All of it was true. I'd started as a skeptic but had turned a firm believer after Raine predicted a death. And she certainly seemed to be keyed into the ghost roaming around my house, even though Edward had never revealed himself to her.

"What a good idea," Kitty said. "I'm sure Lauren is in a terrible way though after her beautiful portrait was destroyed. So be careful. She can be grumpy when she's in bad spirits." She smiled at her play on words, and I'd certainly been on the receiving end of a badly spirited spirit more than once. "Feel free to explore. I've canceled next weekend's guests. Lucy, Wilma and I are just going to relax for a few days."

"That sounds like a good plan," I said. "We'll let you get back to the silver then."

"Let me know if you run into Lauren," she called as we left the dining room.

I motioned for Raine to follow. "I'm going straight for the stairs. I want to look around. Not sure what I'll find but that's the best place to start."

Raine and I turned the corner to the stairs. Angela was staring at her phone as she walked down. She lifted her face and didn't look thrilled to see us. "You're back again, Sunni?" Her tone was almost accusatory. She stopped a few steps up and sighed loudly. "Haven't you bothered Kitty enough? And me? I lost my brother, after all."

"Half brother," I said defensively. Her tone was making me bristle. It wasn't like her to be so harsh.

"Hardly the point. The tragedy is never going to be behind me with this constant search for some mysterious killer. Kenneth fell down the stairs and hit his head. It was an accident. I don't know why this is getting stretched out into a sordid murder investigation."

Raine shot me a sideways glance but wisely kept her comments to herself.

"So your brother's pleas before his fall were just Kenneth talking to himself?"

She blew a frustrated sound from her lips. "The frivolous imaginations of two staff members is not solid evidence for a murder case. Even I know that."

"And the painting? That wasn't a crime either?" I asked.

"Of course it was, but it had nothing to do with us. Who knows, it might even have been Lauren herself. Ghosts can get very mischievous when they're angry, and she must certainly be angry about all the people traipsing through her house this week. Besides, I've already told Kitty to have it appraised so I can reimburse her for the portrait. Barbara is resting right now. The two of us are leaving in the morning."

"That's generous for someone who didn't have anything to do with the damage," I noted. I wanted badly to mention that she must have come into a fortune lately but that might have been pushing it. She'd gotten my hackles up, mostly because I hadn't expected her to be so rude. Why was she was suddenly so keen to get her brother's death behind her?

"Yes, well, I certainly didn't learn generosity from my father or brother." She finished her descent to the landing and swept past us without another word.

Raine and I watched her disappear into the dining room.

"She's sweet," Raine quipped.

I stifled a laugh. "She was the first few times I met her. I wonder what's changed. Or maybe I'm more irritating than I realized."

Raine put her arm around my shoulder as we climbed the stairs. "Nonsense. You're mildly irritating at best. Seems kind of odd that she doesn't want to know exactly how her brother died."

"Yes, it is odd." We reached the top of the stairs, and I looked back down them. Just days earlier, Kenneth had stood right where we stood and taken his last breath before falling and receiving a fatal blow to the head. "Do you sense anything here?" I asked.

Raine took her hand from my shoulder and touched the oak banister. She closed her eyes and grew quiet in concentration. I waited in tense silence for her to pick up something, a vibration, a static charge, something that might let us know that Lauren was near. Edward materialized at will any place in the house. I could only assume the Dandelion ghost had the same abilities.

Raine's head dropped and her fingers squeezed the banister as she ran her hand over it. She was deeply absorbed in her task. I held my breath and waited, certain she was onto something.

Her face popped up. "Nope, not a thing. I'm telling you this ghost exists only in people's imaginations."

"Darn. Not sure what I was hoping for but after that strange interaction on the stairs with Angela, I'm convinced there is more to Kenneth's death than a bad fall. Let's explore."

Kitty had beautifully woven runners down the center of two hallways, each leading to a different side of the house. Polished hardwood floors peeked out from each side of the runners. "Gosh, I wish my floors looked like this already," I said as we strolled down the hallway.

Raine stopped at a small side table that held a porcelain vase with fake roses. "This place sure is spotless. I can practically see myself in these silk flowers."

"I know. It's daunting, to say the least." We reached the end of the hallway. A small white door with a brass handle sat adjacent to the final bedroom door.

Raine laughed. "Is that a door to a dollhouse?"

"You don't know much about old houses. This is a laundry chute. It probably goes all the way down to the basement where there's a laundry basket waiting to catch clothes and linens."

A piece of white fabric was jammed in the closed door. "Only this piece of clothing got caught and never made it to the bottom." I opened the door to free the fabric but something made me grab it and pull it out instead. Much more fabric came behind the piece jammed in the door. By the time I pulled it free, there was a long white dress hanging in front of me.

"Looks like someone's old wedding gown," Raine said. "Sort of a strange thing to shove down a laundry chute."

"I'll say." I handed it to her. "Hold this up for a second. It looks eerily familiar."

Raine held it under her chin and walked along with it like she was on a runway. "Does it suit me?"

"Not particularly. Especially with the yellow beanie."

She reached up to touch the beanie as if she'd forgotten it was there. "Maybe if I put a tiara over the beanie."

As she mused about her fashion statement, I remembered where I'd seen a dress like it.

"Lauren Grace," I said abruptly.

Raine swung around. "Where?"

"No, the dress. It looks a lot like the dress Lauren was wearing in her portrait, the painting that was shredded last night."

Raine handed it back to me. "Not my style after all."

"Let's go downstairs. I need to ask Kitty who the dress belongs to."

Raine raised a brow. "I see little gears turning in that head of yours, friend. What are you up to?"

"It's just a hunch but I think we just uncovered a major clue to solving the murder mystery."

CHAPTER 33

*R*aine trotted behind as I carried the dress down the
stairs and into the dining room. Angela stiffened when
she saw us enter. Kitty was still hunched over a silver bowl,
grinding away with the polishing cloth.

I decided to ignore Angela's skewering gaze and go straight to
Kitty. My footsteps and the rustling of the chiffon dress caught her
attention. She looked up from her task and immediately focused
on the dress.

"What do you have there, Sunni?" Kitty asked. The color
drained from her cheeks. "Why it almost looks as if you're
holding—"

"Lauren Grace's dress?" I asked.

She was stunned silent a moment, then she lifted her face to
me. "Why yes, that's exactly what it looks like."

I held it up for her to get a better look and sensed some hot
tension coming from the next table where Angela was nibbling a
scone. Kenneth's sister had the most to gain from his death, and
she was certainly acting suspiciously.

"Kitty, do you know who this belongs to? A piece of the fabric was sticking out of the door to the laundry chute. I opened it, to free the garment. It seemed like a strange thing to find in the chute. I thought they were generally used for towels and linens."

"Wilma doesn't use the chute at all. She prefers to toss everything in a basket and carry it down to the basement herself." I'd grabbed Kitty's full attention. She put down her polishing cloth and got up from the table to examine the dress. "It's cheaply made," she said on further inspection. "Not expensive, custom finery like Lauren is wearing." Her throat caught a hitch. "I mean was wearing," she said mournfully as if she were talking about the recent passing of a dear friend. Kitty fingered the tiny buttons. "It almost looks like something you'd buy at a costume shop."

"Costume," I repeated the word to myself.

"Gears still grinding," Raine muttered quietly next to me.

"Do you know where the dress came from?" I asked Kitty.

Her chin drew long in consideration. "I've never seen it before in my life."

Wilma walked into the room right then.

"Wilma," Kitty called to her. "Come look at this dress. Do you know how it got into the laundry chute?"

Wilma's brows furrowed while she did the same light touch inspection as Kitty. "I've never seen it before, but it does remind me of the dress in the portrait." Her gaze went instinctively to the mantel but then dropped when the empty wall reminded her of last night's vandalism.

Angela stood up abruptly enough to scrape the chair legs on the floor. "I'll let all of you examine the dress. I'm going up to pack." With that, she hurried out of the room leaving a trail of cool air in her wake.

Raine gave me a conspiratorial wink. She hadn't spoken to Angela much, but you didn't need to know someone to know when they were acting unnecessarily agitated.

"Have you been using the laundry chute?" Kitty asked Wilma.

Wilma shook her head. "Never. I prefer my laundry basket." She turned to me to explain. "I can take it from room to room rather than making constant trips out to the hallway."

"Makes sense," Raine noted.

The kitchen door swung open. Lucy walked out carrying a tray with a scone and coffee. "Wilma, could you run this up to Barbara's room? I don't want the other scones to burn."

Wilma looked at her fingers. They were covered with silver polish. This was my opportunity to have a chat with Barbara.

"I can take it," I volunteered quickly. Without waiting for a response, I walked toward Lucy and took hold of the tray. "Which room is Barbara in?"

"Left at the top of the stairs. Last door on the right," Lucy said. "Thanks and I'll have a fresh batch of cranberry scones in two shakes. That'll take the glum mood out of this room for sure."

Raine pulled up a chair next to Kitty. "I'll stay here. I want to ask Kitty about some of the reported sightings of Lauren Grace. I'm curious to learn more about her."

"*And* you don't want to miss a hot scone," I added.

"Yes, and that too."

"After the Marlon Brando, I'm surprised you have room," I muttered on my way out.

"Always room for baked goods," Raine called to me.

I carried the tray up the stairs and turned left, toward Barbara's room. The second door from the end was just shutting as I reached the hallway. It had to have been Angela's room. As far as I knew, there was no one else staying at the inn. The men had left and it was just Kitty and the staff. And they were all in the dining area. I would have seen her if she had just climbed the stairs. I could only assume she came from a different direction, and the only thing past her room was Barbara's door and the now infamous laundry chute.

I knocked lightly on the door.

"Come in," Barbara called weakly.

I opened the door. Her shock at seeing me carry in her tray couldn't have been more clear. Her skin smoothed like marble, and she blinked a few times to make sure she wasn't imagining it. She was sitting in her bed, propped up against pillows with a book on her lap.

"I hope you don't mind that I carried this in. Lucy and Wilma were both occupied with other tasks, so I volunteered."

"Oh, yes, I—I should have come down myself, but I'm still feeling poorly. This is all such a shock to me."

"I understand completely."

Barbara moved her book, and I set the tray on her lap.

I struck up a conversation, hoping we could talk about Angela. It seemed possible that Barbara knew more than anyone else. She and Angela appeared to be close. I walked over to the tall oak dresser and pretended to admire her silver plated hairbrush and mirror. "These are lovely." I picked up the mirror.

Barbara broke a chunk of scone off. "Aren't they? I found them at an estate sale near my home."

"I guess you and Angela will be heading out soon," I said as I put down the mirror.

"Yes, the sooner we get away from this place, the better." Her shoulders slumped beneath her robe. "It's filled with terrible memories now. I can't wait to leave. As soon as I feel strong enough, I'm going to get up and pack." She motioned to her suitcases sitting on the upholstered dressing bench at the end of the bed.

"Packing is always something I dread." As I spoke, something on the hairbrush caught my eye. I picked up the brush and discretely pulled free the yellow strand of synthetic hair. "I can never seem to fit everything back inside when I'm leaving." I walked over to the suitcases and saw a few of the same yellow strands stuck with static to the sides of one of them.

"I won't have a problem with that now," she said through a sip of coffee. She lowered the cup abruptly. Her eyes rounded as if she wanted to suck the sentence back in.

"Oh, are you leaving with less than you came with?" I asked casually.

Barbara rubbed her forehead. "You know I've got a slight headache. If you don't mind taking this tray back downstairs, I think I'll take a short nap."

I pushed the strand of fake hair into my pocket and walked back to her with a concerned brow. "Can I get you anything? An aspirin, perhaps?"

"No." She practically shoved the tray into my hands. "I just need to rest. Please close the door on your way out." She immediately slipped down on the pillows and pulled the cover over herself as she turned away from me in the bed.

I carried the tray downstairs. Raine, who had cheeks full of scone like a chipmunk, seemed to notice that something was up. She followed me into the kitchen. Lucy was foraging around in the pantry, muttering to herself, giving me a brief opportunity to talk to Raine.

My whisper was well hidden by the roar of the stove hood, where Lucy was cooking a pot of something that smelled delicious.

"I think Barbara is responsible for Kenneth's fall down the stairs," I whispered loudly.

"How do you know?" Raine asked.

Lucy reemerged from the pantry holding a bag of potatoes.

"Lucy, I brought the tray back down. Barbara said she has a headache and wants to rest."

Lucy put her hands on her hips and stared angrily at the barely touched scone. "That woman is as delicate as a lace curtain. Thank you for saving me the trip up those stairs."

"You're welcome." I glanced at the door leading out to the backyard. "Is it all right if I take a stroll through the garden, Lucy? It looks charming."

"Sure thing. And the view is best if you walk along the brick pathway toward the back wall and then up along the maple trees."

"Thanks. I'll do just that." I looked at Raine. "Up for a walk or are you still eating scones?" I leaned closer to her. "I need to call Jackson."

She patted her belly. "I think I've reached my limit for the day. But you go ahead. Kitty and I were having a great conversation about an old house she used to live in as a little girl. Not one ghost but three."

"Go ahead and get back to the discussion then. I'm just going out for a stroll." I headed out the back door. For a moment, I forgot the main purpose for the walk. Kitty's garden was a symmetrical maze of round flower and herb plots, each one organized and neatly planned. The colors of spring and summer were no longer visible, but it was easy to imagine the rainbow of nature that took over the garden during the blooming months. My backyard was not a backyard but a vast open field of grass, weeds and anything else that felt the urge to grow behind the house.

"So much work to be done," I groaned, then snapped out of my defeatist mood and pulled out my phone. After the night before, I was a bit hesitant about calling Jackson, but I was certain he'd be pleased once I told him what I found.

"Hey, Sunni, I was just about to call you. Are you still at Dandelion Inn?"

"Yes, that's what I called you about. I think I've solved the case."

He cleared his throat. "Which case? Applegate's death or the painting?"

"Oops, I forgot all about the painting." I walked to a white wrought iron bench under a maple tree and sat down. "I've got a theory about Kenneth's fall."

"Theories aren't exactly ironclad in court."

"No, there's evidence to go with it, but I don't think this will have anything to do with court. It has to do with heartbreak and desperation and a ghost expert who was not terribly expert."

"Maybe we can wrap all this up. I've got a fingerprint match on the letter opener," Jackson said. "I'm heading your way right now. Should be there in five minutes."

"All right, I'll just sit here in Kitty's garden and lament how far my inn has to go to be civilized enough for human visitors."

CHAPTER 34

*R*aine and Kitty had gotten so involved in their conversation, as I walked through the dining room, my friend didn't even notice me. She'd even picked up a cloth and joined in on the silver polishing session.

I mentioned to Kitty that Detective Jackson was on his way with some information about the painting then I headed out to the front yard to wait for him. I wanted to talk to him before we were inside where others could hear. It was entirely possible that my theory was way off. I certainly didn't want to accuse or offend people until I knew for sure. There was a nice amount of evidence supporting it though, and I was rather pleased with myself for coming up with it.

Jackson's car pulled up in front of the house. I curled my hands to stop the annoying trembling that always started when I was about to come face to face with him. He climbed out of his car and pushed his sunglasses up into his thick hair. His long legs carried him quickly across the lawn to the brick pathway where I was standing.

"Bluebird, I see you're outside enjoying the fresh air."

"Wanted to talk to you first. But before I start, whose finger-prints were on the letter opener?"

"There were two sets of prints. Since we saw her holding it, we can assume one belongs to Wilma. I put the second print into the database and found a match with a federal employee, a postal worker, to be more specific. Barbara Simpson retired from the postal service two years ago. The big question remaining is why would a perfectly sweet ex-postal worker want to shred a painting?"

"I think I might know." I pulled the strand of fake hair from my pocket and held it up in the light.

He squinted at it. "Is that the wig fiber?"

"It sure is. I found it in Barbara's hairbrush. And there were a few strands on her suitcase. I'm fairly certain, if you open her luggage, there will be a wig to go with these strands. And that's not all. Raine and I were snooping around the hallway, and I noticed some fabric sticking out of the laundry chute. I pulled the garment free and discovered it was a long, white dress. It looks like the one Lauren Grace was wearing in her portrait."

"You think Barbara was dressing up to look like Lauren Grace?"

"Yes, exactly."

"Was she trying to scare the group or was she just making sure there was at least one ghostly sighting during their stay at the inn?" he asked.

I glanced back at the house. The light was on in Barbara's room. It seemed she was up and about. I turned back to Jackson. "Barbara was madly in love with Kenneth Applegate, but he hardly paid her any attention at all. At the same time, Kenneth was obsessed with Lauren Grace."

My theory gelled in his mind. "Ah ha, so she dressed up like Lauren to get his attention."

"And she got it all right," I said. "I think the mark on his chest was Barbara trying to grab Kenneth as he fell."

Jackson rubbed his chin. "But if he was in love with Lauren Grace, why was he telling her to go away when he finally met up with her on the stairs?"

"Because, as a few people have pointed out, Raine included, Kenneth Applegate was not a skilled ghost hunter. Something tells me, Barbara's version of the Lauren Grace ghost was his first encounter with a *spirit*."

Jackson nodded. "She tried to touch him. He got scared and stepped back too far. So, in a way, he was scared to death."

"Nice play on words, Detective Jackson. I guess we should go inside and see if the scenario is true."

We walked into the house. It was the second time that day I'd run into the unpleasant side of Angela Applegate. "Poor Kitty," she said in a huff as she came down the stairs. "She is having to put up with so much commotion this week."

Jackson stopped and stared at her. "If by commotion you mean an investigation into your brother's death, than yes, Miss Bloom-field is having a difficult week. But I'm sure she'd like me find out what happened to Kenneth, as well as the painting." He spoke coolly enough that she had no real response except a small huff.

"I'll be gone from here tomorrow," she said curtly. "I've already left word with the coroner on instructions for Kenneth's body. He wanted to be cremated."

"I suppose that is mentioned in his will," Jackson said pointedly.

Her eyes flickered with unease. "Yes, it was part of his estate. If you'll excuse me." She tried to sidle past him.

"Miss Applegate," he said, "can you tell me where Miss Simpson is right now?"

She looked perplexed by the question, and it seemed she didn't want to answer. "She is still upstairs," she said reluctantly.

"If you don't mind, could you tell her to come downstairs and bring her suitcases with her."

Again, she was hesitant. But Jackson's imposing size and the confident way he handled people, made him a hard person to say no to.

"Yes, I'll go upstairs and see if she's dressed." Angela wandered toward the stairs in no particular hurry.

"Dress," I said with a finger snap. "I'll go get the dress I found." I hurried into the dining room. Raine and Kitty had moved on to a pot of tea.

"Kitty, just so you know, Detective Jackson is here." I picked the dress up off the chair. "I'm going to show this to him."

Kitty laughed. "What interest would Detective Jackson have in a dress?"

"Not even his style," Raine quipped. They had a good laugh together as I carried the dress out of the room. If nothing else, it seemed Raine had given Kitty an afternoon off from all her worries. My friend was good at that.

Jackson was still waiting for Barbara to come down the stairs when I returned with the dress. I held it up against me. "What do you think?"

"You'd make an adorable bride."

His comment was so unexpected, words escaped me.

He chuckled. "I'm just kidding around. Sort of." He added cryptically at the end.

I pushed the comment to the back of my mind. "Do you see how similar the dress looks to the one in the portrait?"

"I don't remember too many details about the dress but yes, I can see it."

Tentative footsteps came down the stair. Barbara blanched as white as the dress when she saw it in my hands. She covered her face and sobbed. Angela moved to stand next to her and put her arm around her shoulder.

"Why don't we go into the drawing room," I suggested. "Then Barbara can have a seat."

Angela nodded in agreement and led a shaken Barbara to the drawing room. Jackson and I followed. They had come downstairs without the suitcases but something told me they wouldn't be needed. The floodgates had been opened, and it seemed we were about to hear everything.

Barbara and Angela sat next to each other on the settee near the window, and Jackson and I took the wingback chairs to face them. Jackson didn't say a word. He just leaned forward, resting his forearms on his thighs, to show he was ready to listen.

Angela pulled a tissue from her pocket and handed it to Barbara. She kept a supportive arm around her. She was certainly not upset with Barbara over Kenneth's death. If Angela and Kenneth had different mothers, it was more than plausible that they were never all that close to begin with.

"It was all a terrible mistake," Barbara said through a sniffle. She paused to blow her nose and took a deep breath. "You see, I just wanted him to notice me." She said those words toward me as if it was something we women had in common more than we liked to admit. (She had a good point.) She turned her puffy eyes back to Jackson. "He was so obsessed with that woman," she said it with such derision, one could almost believe that Lauren Grace was alive and well and stealing other women's boyfriends. "It was a silly idea but I thought if I dressed up like Lauren and pretended to be her—"

"You mean Lauren Grace?" Jackson asked.

"Yes, I thought it would be fun and that it might get him to notice me, to look at me the way he was always staring at that blasted portrait."

Jackson and I exchanged glances at her last few words. It seemed Barbara was the painting vandal as well.

Barbara wiped her eyes, but the tears had stopped. She shook her head dejectedly. "It all went so horribly wrong. Kenneth was just reaching the top of the stairs when I came out of my room in a wig and the dress. I reached toward him. Only a few sconces were lit in the hallway, so the light was dim. I thought he would recognize me, but he panicked. He yelled for me to go away and took a sharp step backward. His arms flailed but I was only able to grab a piece of his shirt." She shuddered visibly and took another breath. "The next thing I knew, Kenneth was dead at the bottom of the stairs. I ran back to my room and shut the door. I was so frightened about what I'd done." A dry sob shook her shoulders. "I loved him. I never would have hurt him. But when the police showed up, I was too terrified to say anything."

Angela, who had been sitting silently next to her, spoke up for the first time. "She confessed everything to me on the way to the hospital. I've forgiven her. It was a tragic accident, that's all."

Barbara's nostrils flared. "It was all her fault, that awful Lauren Grace."

"So that's why you destroyed the painting?" I asked. "Revenge?"

Barbara dropped her face in shame. "Yes."

Angela squeezed her shoulders again. "But I'm going to reimburse Kitty for the value of the painting so there won't be any charges."

Jackson nodded. "Then this case is closed. Thank you for letting us know what happened."

The two women got up and shuffled out of the room.

Jackson leaned back and ran his hands over the arms of the wingchair. He rested his head back and turned his face my direction.

"Nice detective work, Bluebird."

I smiled. "Thank you very much."

CHAPTER 35

*H*aving a box of chocolates hand delivered to your door was always extra special. Having a marvelously handsome detective deliver that box of chocolates gave a turbo boost to extra special.

"I just came by to say thank you for your help with the Applegate case." Jackson stood in the front door as he handed me the black velvet box. It was topped with a dazzling gold ribbon. "I did a large amount of mind debate, trying to decide if you were a dark chocolate or milk chocolate kind of girl. Couldn't come to any conclusion, so I bought you both."

I took the box. "You can be sure that if chocolate is the main word, you can place basically any descriptor in front of it and I'll eat it."

"Soo"—he squinted one eye in thought—"Cricket-filled chocolate?"

"No. Even I have my limits." I motioned for him to follow me into the kitchen.

LONDON LOVETT

"I don't want to keep you," he said as he walked behind me. "I can see you're on your way out."

"I've still got a few things to do in the house. But what gave it away? My rustic barn attire?" I placed the chocolate on the counter and waved my hand to highlight my faded jeans that were missing knees and my old sneakers. "I'm just on my way to help my sister, Emily, do farm chores. I find they help me clear my head on the weekend. Nothing like some quality time with chickens, goats and horses."

"That actually sounds more fun than my day. I promised to meet some friends in the city for lunch. Long drive, lots of mindless talk, way too much food and then a long drive back."

"You do have a lot of friends," I noted.

"Yeah, maybe more than I need." We walked back out to the porch and stood face to face, leaning against the railing. His amber eyes were always filled with energy and spirit.

"Thanks again for the chocolate but you really didn't need to. You know how much I love to solve murder mysteries."

Tiny creases formed on one side of his mouth. It was that tilted grin that always took his appeal one step further. "You sure do and you're good at it. Did you get your article written?"

"I did. Barbara allowed me to write the story. I titled it "When Heartbreak Turns to Tragedy".

"Now that's a nice hook. You're too talented for the *Junction Times*."

"So I've been told, but I'm thankful to Parker for giving me the job." I leaned my head toward the house. "You may or may not have noticed but I live in the quintessential *money pit*."

"It does have a way to go before it's like Dandelion Inn."

"That reminds me," I said. "Naturally, I had Kitty's permission to write the story too. She texted me that she's getting tons of reservations based on the article."

"I'm glad for her." Jackson stepped toward me. "And I'm glad you moved into Firefly Junction." He leaned closer.

My heart raced. It seemed I was about to get that kiss. That kiss. I needed to outsmart Edward and his mischief. "Uh, I know this is kind of a weird request but could we take this down to the front yard?"

Jackson blinked those heavy lashes a few times. "All right."

We walked down the steps to the front yard. We were still in full view of the porch. "Maybe over here, out of view of the house. The dogs get kind of protective of me." What a bunch of baloney that was.

"You mean those two dogs standing under that tree harassing a squirrel?" he asked.

I glanced back over my shoulder. My two dogs were never where they were supposed to be. I laughed lightly. "Well then, we moved for nothing. Now where were we?"

I stepped closer. He reached up and lifted my chin with the side of his finger. I closed my eyes and waited.

"No, you know what—" He lowered his hand. "The moment feels kind of forced now. Never good for a first kiss. I'm going to save it for another time." He headed toward his car.

I was disappointed but at the same time, I had to agree. "I guess *then* I'll see what all the hoopla is about," I called.

He glanced back over his shoulder. "No hoopla. Fireworks maybe but no hoopla."

I waved and walked back up to the porch. I watched him climb into his car. I released a soft audible breath as he drove away.

A tongue clucked behind me. "You are easily charmed. One box of chocolates and you're sighing dreamily."

I chuckled as I walked past him to the door. "Yes, the dreamy sigh was all about the chocolates." I walked inside and shut the door.

ABOUT THE AUTHOR

London Lovett is the author of the Firefly Junction and Port Danby Cozy Mystery series. She loves getting caught up in a good mystery and baking delicious new treats!

Subscribe to London's newsletter [londonlovett.com] to never miss an update.

You can also join London for fun discussions, giveaways and more in her **Secret Sleuths** Facebook group.

https://www.facebook.com/groups/londonlovettssecretsleuths/

Instagram @LondonLovettWrites

https://www.londonlovett.com/
londonlovettwrites@gmail.com

Printed in Great Britain
by Amazon

37793172R00118